Concentric Relations: Unknown Ties
Book I, The Concentric Series
Adair Rowan
Midwest Creations Publishing

Midwest Creations Publishing
Faith-Based Fiction

Midwest Creations Publishing
St. Louis, MO 63130
Visit our website at www.midwest-creations-publishing.weebly.com

This is a work of fiction. Names, characters, places and incidents are a product of the author's imagination or are used fictitiously. Any resemblance to actual persons (living or dead), locales, events or establishments is coincidental. The publisher does not have any control over and does not resume responsibility for the author or any third-party (reviewers, bloggers, booksellers, social network etc.) or their content.

Concentric Relations. Book I, The Concentric Series
Copyright ©1997 by Adair Rowan
ISBN-10: 1-7338114-2-7
ISBN-13: 978-1-7338114-2-2

Originally published electronically via KDP by Midwest
Creations Publishing

Acknowledgements

Dedicated to Allison, my queen, my better half.

My sons Grant and newly arrived Gavin. My mom Wonder (and you know you are) for being an awesome mother, prayer warrior and my loudest cheerleader.

My brother John (thanks for getting your shoes wet bro) and sis in law Justine (love you both and there's nothing you can do about it!).

My cousin Denise aka Naptime, aka ladybug, aka pootiehead #1.

To the Sims Family; we've lost a quite a few of our elders and some in our generation, let's make it a point to bridge any gaps and cover one another with prayer.

To my dad Ernest and my Stepmom Doris, thank you for answering the call, it's been a blessing.

To my eldest bro Petey and sis Pat, thank you for visiting with us and encouraging me to use all my talents.

To bro Brian aka Kavlor, keep getting your hustle on bro.

To all my God-family and friends who have continued to encourage me in this endeavor: The Grant and Pryor Families, The Bruners, The Floyds, The Gilmores, The Reeds, The Fords.

To my STLMO peeps, Tay, Mic, JVN, Chris Jordan, Stan and Courtney, and all my former WU friends.

I also want to mention my TCWW family, Pas. West, Sheretta West and the West Family and all my **#IamTCWW** family.

Preface

Advancements in science are stumbled upon; every now and then, some are reproducible and therefore are applied to other areas of life. Whenever anything is perceived as a tactical advantage is identified; the military takes the prototypes. Soldiers have always been the next in line for radical combat training and military experiments.

Since 1949 Roswell, New Mexico, UFO crash, the government has been trying to find a viable way to implement recovered alien technology for the benefit of mankind. The most interesting recovered items, other than the alien creatures themselves were the scraps of lightweight metallic alloys. They behave as if they are organic in origin. Each piece was several times the strength of our strongest metallic composites.

Military scientists have been using the last 50 plus years to examine these artifacts and coax as many secrets out of them as possible. In secret places like Area 51 and Iron Mountain, these materials have been scrutinized. They have been exposed to various degrees of radiation, laser cartography and extreme temperatures. Scientists involved in the examination and research have been stumped as well as surprised by the way these materials respond.

Only during the last twenty or so years have the military scientists learned even a few of their secrets. This came after one specific signal was detected by SETI teams; from all around the world. The signal started out as one long sequence of alpha-numerics. As the weeks went by, the signal changed and became exponentially more complicated.

There were seven distinct packages of information received on Earth. Scientists all around the Earth exchanged the information they could translate from each package until everyone arrived at the same conclusion. There was an intelligent race of creatures located in our galaxy. They were not initially from our galaxy but had traversed the darkness between ours and theirs over several millennia. They were explorers and scientists from a civilization that had long surpassed our current epoch of development and technology. They were offering to observe and guide humanity on a path of similar enlightenment:

The scientific community was in an uproar. There was excitement, anxiety and trepidation. Their presence changed our world for the better. Our technology took leaps and bounds under the guidance of our new friends, yet their presence always seemed to cast a double-edged shadow. On one edge were the positive possibilities. On the other edge was the nagging question: "What will their assistance and guidance cost mankind?" Over twenty years the ozone layer was repaired, environmental pollution and its associated damage was reversed. All these things took place just out of sight of the public. The leaders of all the world governments were forced to unify into one complimentary government to limit the possibility of informational leaks and to strengthen control over the media.

What there was of war, was transformed into a digital, virtual, mental battleground. Each country applied this new framework and developed a mind-to-mind warrior caste. During the next couple of decades, the possibility of nuclear destruction declined, but the warriors who did carry out these battles were nonetheless damaged severely as their mental battles did have physical repercussions. Those who excelled in this new warcraft had the uncanny ability to self-rehabilitate, whereas those who were unable to do so suffered nerve damage, physical paralysis and sometimes death.

This new era was a golden age. Living computer systems, nanotechnology and symbiotic combat technologies consumed the black budget projects within governments.

The Ultra-Knowledgeable Interactive Network or UKNI was one such black budget project. UKNI was constructed after years of research in atomic robotics, and biomechanical theory. It was the only living computer in existence. It had been grown in the cold darkness of space; completely shielded from x-rays and micro-cosmic forces by a two-foot thick coating of AuTi6 (Gold & Titanium alloy) developed in cooperation with a group of the world's most brilliant civilian, military and other scientists.

This system was made somewhat accessible to the public, compartmentally, only after the last war. It is the only computer with complete access to every military installation, personal computer, digi-phone monitor log, and other satellite-linked phones, or remote device. UKNI oversees the seismic activity from each tectonic plate to ocean basin. It also monitors the space within our solar system with electronic fingers and neutrino eyes, a living latticework that would continue to grow in size and intelligence. Conceivably, it could continue to grow indefinitely. It was conscious, having been produced from embryonic fetal tissue; UKNI knew its relation to humans and therefore held strong regard for human life. The public only knew of the system as the latest Global Satellite Communications Network. Therefore, the general public was unaware of the systems full capabilities.

Having no constraints to its intelligence or memory, it became the storage facility for some of the most critical and sensitive information in the world. Thus, UKNI was the caretaker of the most extensive, interactive file of psychiatric cases possible. Some of those black budget projects created publicly available technologies but not many. Mankind knew little of what was happening, and even less of what was to come.

Chapter 1

Personal recording:
July 14, 2017
Dr. Liam Ronaw,
Ph.D. licensed, Florida, PsyDoc.USMC

"The summer of 1995 was a rare one. It still stands out vividly in my mind. The summer of 95' was the summer of my first kiss. Her name was Nicki Lee; I simply called her Nicki, and she was the granddaughter of one of my grandmother's next-door neighbors. Nicki was two years older than I, and a tad bit taller. She was a tomboy too. Nicki beat my behind at almost every physical activity we engaged in, except swimming. She could box, run, and wrestle: like a pro. Nicki was as tough as they come, by any standard.

That's how it happened, I guess. Nicki and I were wrestling in the corn patch behind her granny's house, she shoved me down and pinned me. We both laughed for a few seconds, and then, for some reason, things weren't so funny anymore. In fact, they were very serious. Our eyes locked in a gaze and I could feel the hair on the back of my neck as it stood on end and my heart began to pound as if it was about to burst. My palms got clammy as the thought of kissing ran through my mind. Gently she pressed her lips firmly against mine. Such softness; such sweetness with a hint of peppermint. Though it was but a brief moment, it felt as if time stopped for an eternity. The air seemed so heavy that for a moment I couldn't breathe; but in an instant, it was all over. Excitement overwhelmed me for a moment, and then Nicki rolled away from me with a devilish smirk on her face. I was somewhat puzzled by her expression until she punched me in the stomach. The wind fled my lungs in a quick gasp of confusion as I crumbled to my knees. I didn't attempt to speak until the air began to return to my burning lungs.

Once I caught my breath, I asked her, "Why'd you punch me?"

With a smirk Nicki responded, "I don't want you to think that I'm getting soft on you."

She smiled and walked away. That moment was pretty romantic, though fleeting. Well, I guess that was about as romantic as it gets when you're twelve years old.

There was a brief pause in the voice on the recording before it continued.

"The second event of that summer was my family reunion. I fondly named it the Reunion Extreme, largely because nineteen ninety-five was the first summer in 5 years that my entire family had been able to get together all at once. It was the most breathtaking sight to behold, especially for a 12-year-old kid. There were roughly two hundred individuals present at this gathering. The ages varied and ideals varied greatly.

There were too many names to remember and I'm certain that I lost a million brain-cells trying to keep up. There was cousin Sputnik; back then I didn't understand why they called him that, but I know now that it was a joke about the shape of his head. He was ten or twelve years older than me and ran his own carpet and upholstery cleaning service. Then there was old Uncle Bird, who always had a hilarious childhood story about the crazy games he and my mom played. I remember him telling me that one time when they were playing cowboys and Indians, he almost died from a knife injury accidentally inflicted by her. They were using real knives and he got cut across his tummy. Boy did my granny wear my mom's bottom out that night after my uncle was stitched up. This warm gathering was on my grandmother Betty-Mae's farm.

I'd never been on a farm before; I mean a real farm, not one of those touristy places like Grant's Farm where you don't actually do anything but gawk at the animals and pass on through. Seeing cows, hens, and chickens scattering about was very exhilarating. I felt like a real cowboy. I chased the chickens for hours and milked a real cow; which felt very strange. I was familiar, mainly, with the hustle and bustle of city life and the laziness also associated with it. Remote controlled TV's, and computers were the most intriguing things I'd ever known to exist. Of course, I knew through reading, what farm life was about, but to experience it for a whole week was like giving a convict keys to a brand-new Porsche and saying you can get in but don't go anywhere.

The day started out as what I assumed was standard on a farm. Up at the crack of dawn, we were all awakened by the sharp shrieking of Lizzie, the eldest and loudest of all the roosters that took up residence on Granny's farm. Granny and a number of my aunts and uncles got up early and fixed a monstrous breakfast of bacon, sausage, French toast, biscuits-n-gravy, omelets, cinnamon rolls and freshly squeezed orange juice. I ate so much that I thought my stomach would burst forth and spew an ocean of food. In the city, most families tend to go to sleep after such a meal, but not in the country. We had to help out with the chores associated with farm life. I used to think that farm life was easy, of course, all I had to draw from was what I'd seen on TV shows and read in books, but I sure found out that you never know until you actually try.

The cows were led to the pasture, the horses groomed, the pigs slopped, and all eggs were gathered from the henhouse. Once all the chores were done, the children were allowed to run and play like prairie dogs throughout the cornfields. Granny didn't sit around and wait for things to get done either, she rolled up her sleeves and got dirty with the rest of us. That ninety-some-odd-year-old woman amazed me; she was wide-eyed and bushy tailed. Thinking back, I just now realize, how much I miss her, she was such an interesting person and a joy to be around.

Later that night I snuck down to the stables and went for a horseback ride on the most beautiful horse in Granny's stable. His name was Quicksilver, he was a purebred mustang according to the stable hands. His stature alone made him stand out from the others in the stable. His stride and power made him one of a kind. Most of the family was very wary of Q, as I affectionately called him. Rumor had it that the horse dragged a man an entire mile at full gallop down a dirt road before stopping. I think that the man must have done something really ornery to Q because he never displayed that evil streak they kept talking about around me. I thought Q was the coolest. He was coal black except for his silver tipped ears, and a dash of silver underneath his chin.

After a long excursion around the property, I rode Q back to the stables, brushed him down and watered him. Once Q was hitched, I went for a dip in the pond that rested directly in front of the house. The driveway enveloped the pond like a lover holding the object of affection in a feverish embrace. The grown-ups played volleyball off the side of the house while Granny; along with her brothers and sisters played horseshoes, a game I never really saw any purpose in playing.

Dinner was equally as magnificent as breakfast, and afterward, most of the family gathered around the back of the house to play cards, drink, smoke, and shoot the breeze. The rest of the evening lolled on by. The sunset was so beautiful. I remember it vividly for its hues of orange and soft reds. Once the sun succumbed to the moons evening strength, most of the family went indoors to lounge around. I, however, sat out on the porch in Granny's favorite rocking chair and enjoyed the fresh, sweet, country air.

It was so relaxing, the gentle whisper of the breeze as it brushed around many different places throughout the cornfield. This was the start of my most interesting memory from the reunion. It was about this time that Jasmine, Granny's rusty colored husky that had been her companion for years, came wandering out from the fields from a day full of work and play, chasing rodents away from the harvest. She came up to the porch and propped herself up as if she was waiting for some attention. I eased out of the rocking chair and stroked her fur. She panted, and I tell you, if I didn't know any better, I'd swear that I saw that old girl grin. Jasmine hopped upon the footstool next to the rocking chair and positioned herself comfortably. She laid her head in my lap, which was really cool considering I'd always wanted a dog.

You know to this day, as I recall those few,

wonderful days I spent on the farm I don't recollect ever seeing a more lovely view of the stars in my life. It was great until Jasmine suddenly pulled her head up and began gazing back and forth over the fields. She stared intensely as if trying to see something in the distance. Observing her unusual behavior, I could tell that something had ruffled her fur and I too, began to look; hoping that my sight was better than hers and that I could see what it was. I had no clue what she could see and grew bored shortly after that, but Jasmine continued with intense interest. After about fifteen minutes she leapt up from the stool, cleared the porch steps in a single bound and disappeared into the darkness. She usually never ran off into the fields at night, at least not since I had been there.

Another thing I figured was odd was that Jasmines didn't bark. At first, I thought that she was off chasing a bunny that had been dumb enough to try and make off with some corn by scrambling through the underbrush, but again there was no barking. I called her a few times, to see if she'd come back, but she never made a sound. That didn't sit well with me; in fact, it made me begin to worry. What if she'd been bitten by a rattler or had fallen into some unnoticed hole out in the fields. I couldn't dare wait until the morning when it could possibly be too late, so I snatched up a flashlight, one of the many Granny had stashed all about the house and ran toward the fields after her. My mind raced with possibilities. Granny would be crushed if her dog was injured.

I entered the darkness of the cornfield, slowly and stealthily, listening for noises that could direct me to Jasmine's whereabouts. I heard the annoying rubbing sound that crickets make; it was so overpowering and came from all directions. I could smell the dampness of the soil, the sweetness of the cornstalks; I could hear the crunching of fallen leaves beneath my feet as I ran. I had only been in the fields fifteen minutes (according to my Trimecca) before my flashlight abruptly stopped working.

"So much for trusty," I thought to myself.

Then things really began to get weird, or even eerie. The field fell deafly silent. The crickets no longer made a sound; even the distant cattle had no voices. Out of nowhere there was warmth, which seemed to pulse all around me. I smelled no smoke, saw no flames, but I still felt the heat. It was kind of like the rippling of a pond when the surface has been touched. It pulsed and passed over me and over again like a wave on the seashore. I looked around more frantically for Jasmine, I screamed out her name, but to no avail. My heart began to pound as sweat trickled down my forehead and slithered down my back. I wasn't sure what caused it, was it the heat or dread over what could've happened to Jasmine.

After I'd progressed a few yards, there was a soft glow that emanated from the sky. No; not from the sky at all, but from two clouds. They moved about sporadically in the sky and were moving too fast to be what they seemed. I realized that I was still walking and stopped just inches from stepping into a hole that would've broken my ankle or leg.

But I didn't care. I was mesmerized by those clouds! The first cloud had a pinkish glow about it, and the other was slightly green. It appeared to me that the green cloud was following the pink one. *So, now clouds were chasing each other?* I thought, *Whew, I must've been dreaming.* I 'd never seen clouds glow except when they were lit up by lightning dancing within.

Then just as suddenly as it all began, it was all over. I remember groggily waking up on Granny's porch, in her chair with Jasmine beside me. I'd been so tired. I thought to myself,

"I've got to stop eating so much before going to sleep; it causes the weirdest dreams. I remembered thinking; *Hey I should write this down; this would make a great science fiction story about abductions someday."*

I never gave much thought to what had happened to me that summer night until I was much older, out of college and running my own psychiatry practice."

Adair Rowan

Chapter 2

Present Day

It was a Friday, in July of 2017 and the day was rather uneventful as usual. It offered less excitement than a ham sandwich does for a pig breeder.

Why? Maybe it was the steady stream of boring clients every Friday. Dr. Ronaw began to feel as if he wasn't accomplishing anything. Sure, he was helping some people out, you know the ones that feel nobody listens to them, even though they seem to go on in a tireless repetitive loop about nothing most of the time. These people had an exaggerated view of their self-importance. Twenty plus years of the same thing began to put him to sleep.

The only thing new that was on the agenda for that day was a new referral. An associate from college was sending a referral to him. The new client's name was Karliece Thompson: a twenty-seven-year-old, master-virtual-data entry clerk and part-time teacher. She was about five foot six, and approximately one hundred thirty-five pounds, with long sandy brown hair. Her figure was unmistakably that of a woman who took her physical health seriously. When she entered the office, he had a sudden feeling of déjà vu. Something about her undeniably sparked his curiosity.

Karliece's story initially started like most Friday clients. The normal stressors associated with confrontations from daily interactions with different associates at work. He initially thought, "That's it," and was intending to suggest the usual self-indulgent treatment that neglected people always wished for.

"I've had some rather perplexing dreams," Karliece began, "for the past six or seven months. I really don't know how to get into this."

"Well Karliece," Ronaw interjected, "just take your time."

She sat quietly for a few moments, as various expressions whisked across her face.

Of course, she's hesitant with the details, she doesn't know you; you haven't built a relationship with her yet, Ronaw thought to himself.

Her expression appeared to be apprehensive, so he suggested,

"Why don't we stick a pin there, and just talk for a while?"

"I don't know..." She responded in a subdued fashion.

"I want to give you a chance to get familiar with me. I want you to feel relaxed and comfortable. Ultimately, I will be able to assist you in identifying and overcoming whatever it is that has been bothering you." Ronaw stated, his tone soothing.

Their meeting progressing, he attempted to break down the reluctance she was feeling. Telling her a few things about himself, he hoped that it would be enough to help her relax and let her guard down. They spoke about the broadest of topics from music to quantum physics. Her interest in quantum physics was what struck him as rather odd given the fact that nothing in her file hinted at any interest in such topics, but as he would later find out, there was more to this young lady than met the eye.

As they talked about Ronaw's athletic ties to Saint Louis University (he was a former college basketball team captain and power forward that led the varsity basketball team to two consecutive championship titles), she mentioned some specifics from the game; an indication to Ronaw that she was an avid sports fan. Karliece loosened up at their shared interest, although not much more, and began to share more details about her dreams.

Personal recording:
July 24, 2017
Dr. Liam Ronaw,
Ph.D. licensed, Florida, PsyDoc.USMC

(Karliece) "I've been having the same dream over and over. In the dream, I saw a dog. The dog was running through a field on a farm. The dream was weird to me because it was absolutely pitch black in the field, but it was like I could see everything in perfect detail."

(Ronaw) "That's the beauty of dreams, anything you see will be in detail due to your mind making your surroundings seem familiar and therefore natural."

(Karliece) "Well, it was a pretty nice-sized farm with a pond directly in front of the house, and there was a driveway encircling the pond directly in front of the house. I remember… a rocking chair on the porch. Inside the house was a woman, an old woman, ancient but jovial and energetic. There were many people there too, but very few of them stood out in my mind. Actually, only one does, a little boy who was chasing the dog. The dog was a husky of some sort, possibly a Siberian, its fur was a reddish, rusty color. I assume that was either its natural color or a change brought on by age. The dog was very energetic despite having a slight limp as if she had been in an accident at one time or another."

While listening Ronaw thought to himself, "Wait, what was that she said, something about a little boy who was chasing a dog through a cornfield in total darkness." At first, he was just stunned, and then he was overwhelmed with more than simple curiosity. He was glad that he had immediately begun recording his sessions with Karliece to refer to them later and try to make sense of all she was saying. Her remarks had thrown his mind into a flurry of thoughts; thus, he couldn't focus on the meat of her problem.

At this point, he suggested, "Why don't we take a break and get a bite to eat?"
Karliece responded cautiously, "Is this something that we can do? I mean go off the premises for a session?"

"Well yes, we can," Ronaw answered in his moderated "therapist" tone. "It's the same as me coming to wherever you are for a session, only this time you get to eat. Plus, I have some free time before my next client due to a reschedule. I thought this would be good and perhaps assuage any additional apprehensions you may have about opening up to me as your therapist."
Karliece appeared to weigh his suggestion before calmly responded, "Well I did skip breakfast, so why not?"

They compromised on a small neighborhood diner, which was only a brief walk from the practice. A casual spot where they could both eat a light yet filling meal.

Karliece wanted to discuss the ramifications behind a new amendment that was being voted on in the Senate for the legal usage of biometry in the health industry. Biometry was the replacement of mal-formed or missing appendages on the human body with robotic implants. It was a discussion that kept them off the subject of her immediate problems and allowed them to converse freely without having to worry about anybody around them knowing that she was a client. They discussed the pros and cons of the issue during their meal.

As they were standing up from their table and preparing to leave, a sturdily built gentleman strode into the diner and caught Karliece's eye. The young man was athletically dressed wearing snug, runner shorts and Nike cross-trainers. Physiologically he seemed to be in good shape, her gaze attesting to this as it caressed his frame from top to bottom when he sat down at his table. He wasn't paying them any attention until he happened to glance up and catch Karliece staring at him. He didn't rise from his seat, but he too seemed a bit shaken. His face displayed mixed emotions like he was trying to recall where he'd seen her face. He just sat there and glared in their direction as they were leaving.

Ronaw gently pulled on her sleeve and guided her out of the restaurant. She appeared to be somewhat dazed. She finally began to speak when there were about halfway to his office, and when she did, her words spewed forth quickly and a bit incoherently. Ronaw asked her to repeat what she said; this time slower so that he could understand.

What she said next, "That man, I've seen him before, I just can't place it but I know that I know him from somewhere...." set off a strange series of events in his life.

Adair Rowan

Chapter 3

On July 28th, Ronaw received a call from his long-time friend and colleague, Dustin Relano Ph.D., of Tennessee. Ronaw answered the call casually, "Hey Dustin, how are you, my friend?"

"Aw man, you know... just running around like a chicken with my head cut off. You know how I do." He joked before his tone became more serious.

"Listen, Liam, I have a family of clients, the Canton family, who have recently resettled to your area and as I don't plan on moving, I was wondering if you would uh."

Finishing his sentence, Ronaw calmly added, "You were wondering if I could fit them into my caseload?"

Dustin paused briefly and in a relieved tone said, "Yes, exactly my brother, their case is an interesting one. I'm forwarding you the details, oh, and by the way, can you keep your logged notes very uh, discrete?"

Sarcastically, Ronaw responded, "My name is Liam Discrete Ronaw, of course, you know me man, my first duty is to the client."

They both laughed briefly before Dustin said, "Listen brother, I have another client coming in about five minutes, but I will try to catch up with you in a few days when I have some free time."

Ronaw's interest was ignited so he could not wait to pry open the file. Excitedly he responded, "That's alright with me brother, do me a favor and give your wife and family my love."

In a very calm tone, Dustin replied, "Will do bro, take care and I will talk with you soon."

The call ended just as the digital file hit Ronaw's email. He opened the file and sent it to the printer while he took a quick bathroom break. Upon his return, he began to leaf through the Canton files. This family of four was having some problems. They had a long history of stress-related symptoms, complicated by some form of undetermined paranoia. They also had some instances in which they could not account for their whereabouts or activities for varying lengths of time.

The eldest was Julius Canton, a fifty-six-year-old gentleman. He was a multi-faceted individual; a former cyber-soldier who maintained his top physical and mental health. Julius was an exemplary officer in an elite core of cyber-soldiers as the commander of the Omega Squadron. The Omega squadron earned fame across the nation from their fierce fighting techniques, ingenuity and "never say die" attitude.

Because of Julius leading his team to countless victories, there were forty-eight battles recorded as their total number of missions with minimal casualties that included two of his fifteen-man squad and a few soldiers that suffered slight nerve damage and post-traumatic symptoms. Julius prided the squad's vigilance and ability to neutralize the enemy for successfully preventing more death and instances of mental and nerve damage to either side.

The squad's two losses happened in the last battle that they faced. Julius never forgave himself for those, even when he knew that it wasn't his fault; nor was it in his power to prevent, unless they wished to forfeit the battle that would have left the world in the hands of a group of nations bent on domination.

The present society had joined together peacefully, eliminating many of the problems suffered in the 20th Century. Julius learned to live with what he felt was a disgrace, as he called it, and did everything he could think of to make the lives of the individuals who had given their minds and futures while under his command.

Upon exiting the military, he dived headfirst into religion and became an exemplary leader in his community. He was a deacon in the church he came to call home. When charities arose, no matter how big or small, he always led the way. His gifts were always given whether he was financially stable or not.

During his most recent years outside of the service, he began to have nightmares and dreams about a time before his veteran years. His flashbacks always involved, as noted within his heavily redacted military records, something within the shadows. Whatever it was, had many eyes and limbs waiting with a heavy, almost acrid air of malevolence. The other dreams he had always involved some type of transfiguration while submerged under water.

Maudine, Julius' wife, was a woman to be reckoned with. She was in her mid-fifties also but performed her duties of wife, deaconess, community activist, and mother in such a manner that she was envied by all her peers. She was also a partner in Canton Tailoring, a business that her husband had built from the ground up after the war. She could work a needle so well that clothes felt like a second skin.

She was a brilliant, exuberant and resourceful woman indeed. She was a member of multiple boards and church ministries that it was mind-boggling how she found the time for them all. She too, however, exhibited similar symptoms of restlessness that she attributed to sleepless nights resulting from nightmares. Her dreams were more focused and detailed than those of her husband. She always dreamt of an underwater tunnel, which appeared to end at a point of light some considerable distance away. She too, spoke of something watching, something she could only describe as the embodiment of evil, waiting off in the shadows. Getting to the bottom of this mystery was going to be interesting.

Their son Junior or Julius Jr. seemed to take after his father. At thirty-two years of age, he had achieved financial gravitas and was a leader in academic studies. He started out in real estate, as well as having, obtained his Ph.D. in the arts. He used his hunger for knowledge and security to drive himself past the limits of even the most highly educated. The only setback Junior endured was fatigue. According to his file, he always had a history of nightmares for as long as he could remember, and they all involved something writhing in the shadows making a maddening clicking noise. What he could recall from his dreams, he described as, "Something in the shadows that was dangerous. Its multiple eyes gave off a soft pale red glow."

The last member of the Canton clan was Gina. She was thirty years old, beautiful, and very adept in the sciences. She had already achieved a Bio-Master, Captain in the Marines Health Corps division. This was not an easy thing to do, let alone achieve in less than ten years of service; on top of that being female did not accelerate her advancements. She was incredibly detailed and carefully documented everything she did, making sure that any accolades for her accomplishments could not be placed elsewhere. Her successes were known worldwide, first by the development of the HX retrovirus, which all but wiped out the HIV plague that menaced the world for thirty plus years. At one time in history, it had been so bad that the health commissions of every country had to regulate the process of procreation.

An extensive screening was done which took years to make sure that the possibility of infection by the HIV organisms was possible. Many people lost interest in the search for a cure and the world's population dwindled down to little to a little more than half of what it was during the latter two decades of the twentieth century.

She was also the first woman to localize, label, and deactivate that little bug that used to be known as the common cold. Gina's talents weren't limited to the medical field. She also had an interest in geography and precious metals. Gina was the only member of the family that suffered psychogenic fugue, not of anything that pertained to reality it seemed. She seemed to have a form of amnesia that only pertained to her dream state. (Not like most people, who could remember bits and pieces of a dream.)

He had to keep his notes about this family's case up to date. What they were describing sounded familiar as he began to look into the database for any files resembling theirs. For some unknown reason, he even consulted his own diary, for any correlating observations. His focus was to help them find the underlying issues that propelled them to work so vehemently, for their sanity.

The file contained an audio recording of a hypnotic regression session with Gina

Transcript of Client Gina Canton recording:

"Off the coast of Florida, I was floating through the air...gliding along the Florida Keys for a while and must've drifted away from them. There was nothing but ocean, calming, cool, beautiful, blue, ocean. I could hear the call of the dolphins as they clicked and spoke to one another miles and miles apart. The song of the whales; usually so alien to my ears, seemed to give directions. Their song evoked feelings of longing, frustration, confusion, love, which led to some sort of understanding within my own mind. I don't know how far I floated, but I saw something protruding from the waters of the ocean.

As I drifted closer, I realized it was an island. I had some control over my direction because, with a thought, I flew towards it for a better look. I also flew higher for an overhead view. What I saw was amazing. It was simple, yet implausible for the mind to accept. It wasn't one island at all. There were actually two islands, or shall I say an island and an isle. One was within the other. Both were surrounded by water. A solid land mass surrounded by water which was then surrounded by a donut-shaped, slowly revolving land mass. I've never seen anything like it, nor imagined it. I still have never seen anything remotely like that in my life."

Ronaw targeted in on the details and clarity with which she described her course and what she had seen. Now, taking this into account, and thinking of the rest of her family and the resemblance of Karliece's descriptions, he could not ignore the possibility that there was some sort of a connection between the Cantons and her.

There was also the similarity of other details from her file and several other new clients that made him begin to wonder just how many of them may share a common root problem or issue that he needed to pinpoint. After checking his mental notes and coming up with too many coincidences, he decided to do his own private eye work.

Chapter 4

The rest of his clients, all the dull ones, were on a sort of weekly routine. He did not believe in whimsically prescribing drugs for patients who didn't have a chemical imbalance. These clients were, more often than naught, satisfied with a simple prescription of sun, fun, and self-indulgence. So they did not seem to notice when he began adjusting their session times. Once the client left, he logged in to a secure portal using his virtual reality network during the additional time. He spent the extra time gliding through the most extensive database in the world. This was only available to a select number of Psychiatrists, Psychologists & Psychotherapists with Psycorp military clearance. This database was within a living fully autonomous bio-computer system known as UKNI.

Having no memory constraints, UKNI became the storage facility for some of the most critical and sensitive information in the world. Thus UKNI was the caretaker of the most extensive, interactive file of psychiatric cases possible. Ronaw used this to search for other potential cases resembling the ones he had recently been exposed to.

He knew that all the top Psy-Docs,

periodically uploaded notes into UKNI to allow input and consultation from other professionals, he'd long since given up the idea that one opinion was all it took to diagnose a patient's illness.

Setting the parameters, he made a formal inquiry of UKNI. Once the portal indicated that the search was proceeding, he settled into a virtual visual relaxation program. Not much time had passed when the records found icon appeared within his virtual headset.

UKNI was thorough. UKNI limited the cases to those with very strict correlations to the case details that were entered and displayed with a list of approximately twenty-five cases. These cases ran the gamut, which included families, and singles from all walks of life, UKNI also, highlighted info about time-gaps, deep-seated unexplained fears of the shadows and detailed dreams about water and tunnels.

It took him two days, wired up on Vivi-nox, to sort through the files highlighted by the UKNI global access directory, and to recover, summarize and locate all of the persons, which were noted in the data. Nevertheless, the initial legwork was complete. He took the rest of the night to rehydrate and catch up on needed rest.

The next morning, he scanned each file again and filtered out more cases until even more similarities between these individuals became apparent. Most of them had been born and grew up, according to the records, within a sixty-mile vicinity his late grandmother's farm.

At first, he thought that it must be just some sort of coincidence, but then he found something else that knocked that idea out of the ballpark. Each and every one of these people was enlisted under the care of one of five retired civilians, yet privately contracted military doctors.

The only thing that was odder than a group of retired, military, master physicians was the fact that there was no documentation of any serious or long-term health problems within this entire group. This simply captivated him, so he decided he would try to call up the doctors and do a little snooping around.

He reached out to what was listed as the Exclusive Intellectuals clinic and was connected to Dr. Smith, the administrator of this medical group. After informing Dr. Smith that a few of his former clients had recently become clients at his own practice, he said: "I was doing a professional check, hoping to find out any additional information that one doctor would be willing to share with another."

Dr. Smith was a bit, apprehensive but professional, he requested, "Please forward your credentials for verification." He sternly indicated, "Should your clearance be verified, then and only then will I release details on a former clients case. Oh, and please include any signed release of information documentation from said clients, so that we can confirm them against our files. I will get back to you once this information has been vetted."

There was a two-day gap between that phone interaction and the follow-up discourse. Once Ronaw passed the vetting, proving to Smith that he was indeed, who he claimed to be, Smith was more open and very civil as Ronaw explained.

"There are several families that I have come across who have an interesting connection. They all originate from the same area and share common brief ailments as well as, they were all treated by your facility."

Over a three to six-hour time span, Smith only spoke vaguely and guardedly about those cases mentioned. This struck Ronaw as sort of odd at first, but since his curiosity was peaked, he allowed Smith to continue before asking definitive questions.

"These clients had remarkable healing ability. I've never seen anything like it." Smith sputtered excitedly and went on to cite one particular example.

"One summer, about eight years ago I got most of them together for a sort of client, thank you-gathering. During this occasion, some of the children were playing cowboys and Indians through the hallways of the banquet building. It just so happened that a child was running close to the wall and ran unexpectedly into a door just as it was being flung open. The child that collided with the door was left with a broken arm. Most children would fall out on the floor in pain and scream until the parents came rushing forth. This child didn't. The child simply got up and awkwardly walked back towards mom and dad. Another child on the premises alerted me to what had happened, and I went to offer my assistance. I examined the child and was sure that his arm was broken in two places and his shoulder was dislocated. I called the paramedics and immediately had him taken to a local hospital. The child's breaks were clean with no sign of radial fragmentation, so when we got to the hospital, I asked for X-rays to make an estimate on how long he would need a cast and see what type of damage might ensue when we popped the shoulder back into location. When the X-rays came back and I examined them closely, I found that the shoulder was already relocated. It seemed as if I had misdiagnosed my patient's broken arm. I also assessed that the breaks were clean, but an MRI scan indicated that the mending process of the child's bones was almost complete. Now I realize that, under stress, your mind can play tricks on you, but not to this extreme. I had no way to explain the rapid recovery, so I took a few blood samples for later testing. What I discovered amazes me to this day, and I've never told anyone of the results, not even my current employers."

Ronaw needed and wanted to know more because if he didn't, he felt as if he would burst like a packed piñata struck by a baseball bat. So, he asked, "What did you find out?"

Dr. Smith was silent for a moment. Then, taking a deep breath, he spewed like a volcano, "I'm not sure how to explain it, but the child's blood work wasn't normal, I mean it had some substances within it that we just could not identify."

"What do you mean by substances that you could not identify?" Ronaw asked.

He responded eagerly, "I mean there were some trace elements and compounds that just didn't make sense, so I... Click. Click... buzz." The call was abruptly terminated.

Stunned that the call was cut off Ronaw was stumped and wondered how the line could've been breached since the installation of LOTN (Laser Optic Transceiver Nodules), getting disconnected just did not happen anymore. L.O.T.N. continually tracks the digital satellite communication grid in real time.

At first, he thought, maybe there was something wrong with the line he was using so he attempted to call Dr. Smith back to follow up, but the call would not go through. He waited a while and tried again but to no avail. The line was totally wiped out. He attempted to query UKNI-net to find out what happened to his call that day, only to be informed that his security level clearance would not allow him access and that in itself struck him as rather strange.

He made a mental note to return to this issue later because there was more than enough to research.

Chapter 5

A few days later Ronaw was involved in a session with Karliece and she was using a graphics data board linked with his computer system to compile descriptions of the faces she remembered from her dreams.

The face that stood out from them all was the face of a young man. It seemed to be the face of the man they saw in the restaurant a few weeks earlier. She had several faces that she remembered in enough detail to make complete pictures. Ronaw used a virtual drive to store the data she generated. When her time was up, she left his office in a jovial mood.

As she was exiting, she smiled, "I finally feel as if I am getting somewhere with what's been bothering me for years. Having no real idea as to what it is, I am just happy we are doing something to figure it out."

The name that appeared to match the description given by Karliece contained a diverse portfolio. His name was Lahmed Lakur. He was considered a genius on Wall Street and had been on the cover of Time, Newsweek and several of the nations' leading business publications. In his late twenties, he 'd done very well for himself, making his first million before he was seventeen.

His background before that time was a bit shaky, but from that point on, he was in the spotlight and definitely holding the image true.

The only things which were known for sure about Lakur's past were that his parents had suddenly disappeared while on a vacation trip slightly outside of the Bermuda Triangle three weeks before his tenth birthday, and until his sudden appearance in the limelight, he was rarely seen or heard of. The only real records of his existence were his occasional doctors' visits, odd jobs, and educational endeavors.

Lakur graduated from Harvard in a record time of two and a half years with a Ph.D. in fiscal management, an MD in accounting, and a minor in the sciences. After that, he used his millions earned from an investor by betting on the lucrativeness of a specific commodity to start his own video production company. Within three years Lakur had opened three additional offices; one on the east coast and two on the west coast (in Washington and the other in California).

He spent most of his time flying from coast to coast monitoring his businesses and promoting the funding of housing communities located all over the country. They were constructed for the homeless and jobless which gave them high-quality shelter and training to become an asset to society rather than a societal burden. As a result, a few of those housing community people became successful contributed much-needed support to that same program.

He was now taking up residence in his retreat in the southeastern area of Florida. His ventures in and around that area had only recently been in the news. He had recently expunged an enormous amount of money in aquatic research. While that wouldn't concern most people, something about that endeavor just bugged the hell out of Ronaw.

Deciding to take a weekend trip to meet this industrious young man in person, Ronaw contacted Lakur's secretary hoping to find an appropriate time only to find that Mr. Lakur had already told his secretary that he would be calling. At first, it seemed like the young man had ESP, but after thinking for a moment, Ronaw realized that a man in his position must have someone, if not a team of individuals, monitoring who was trying to find out about him.

The past few weeks had been exhilarating and exhausting. Ronaw chartered a private plane (a perk of having the Psycorp licensing) so that he could ride in comfort. Not wanting to be disturbed while he caught up on some much-needed sleep, Ronaw left word at his office to forward client calls to his messaging service during the flight.

It was halfway through his flight that he woke up with a vague feeling of being watched. He didn't know why he felt this way, but he did. Ronaw had learned to follow his gut at an early age, so he squinted out of the window of the plane but saw nothing. *This case must be working on my imagination*, he thought to himself.

As the jet landed, Ronaw turned on his phone and found a message from the elder Canton requesting a callback. He decided to call Mr. Canton while the plane was taxying to the gate.

When Mr. Canton answered his call, he sounded a little frantic. "I had another odd dream. There was a swarm of these vile creatures! They were chasing me in a place that was lush and green. It was humid. Wherever I was, it wasn't on Earth, and I know that"

His statement mystified Ronaw, so he paused before asking, "What do you mean by it wasn't on Earth?"

Mr. Canton paused for a second to catch his breath and replied, "Well . . . for one, the sky was different."

"How was it different?"

"I mean, there was no moon, and no stars as far as I can remember," he grunted as he cleared his throat.

"I saw a sea of winged creatures that looked like. . . like nothing I've ever seen before. They were huge, but in a funny sort of way, they were graceful. Their eyes were not set within skulls, like a normal animal here. They actually had nothing that even resembled a skull, now that I think about it. Where a head and torso should have been, there was a sort of gelatinous bubble about the size of a watermelon. Within this mass was what I could only say was a bioluminescent soup, which reacted with each movement of the creature's wings. They flew around me and close to me, as their bodies radiated beautiful colors. They became darker and dimmer looking the slower they moved. Then they faded to complete blackness. The one closest to me was so black that it seemed to be drawing all the surrounding light into it. It landed about ten feet from me and slithered around on what I imagine was its belly. The underside left a semi-slimy substance as it moved slowly across the ground. It's head was almost glowing as it came toward me. The funny thing was that I got the feeling that this creature was warning me of some impending danger. Then I heard them!"

"Them! Who, more of these creatures?" Ronaw asked.

"Hell no! Naw, these new things were something else. What I saw would make a marine piss on himself."

"What did you see Mr. Canton?"

"They were stream-lined killing machines." He said matter-of-factly.

"Excuse me?" Ronaw inquired.

"Look here Doc, I'm getting old, but I'm not senile yet. I tell you that there were so many eyes on the heads of these things; I imagine that they could see every angle and direction at once. There were about four arm-like appendages and I swear I've never seen anything like it. If they didn't sound like huge lawnmowers while in flight, I never would have known they were coming. As soon as they were above their prey, their wings folded and dived down like a hawk on an unsuspecting rodent. They pounce on their prey, the first creatures, without a sound. Their movements were silent, deliberate, and deadly. If I hadn't been facing it during its attempt, I bet it would've snatched me up in the multiple arms that came out of what I can only describe as the chest. They were kind of like a praying mantis. They filled the sky and the land for as far as the eye could see. There was something else kind of strange also about my recollection of this incident."

"Like what?" Ronaw asked

"Well, I was seeing in three different directions at once. Don't ask me to explain more than that Doc." The line grew quiet.

"All right Mr. Canton, if anything more comes to mind please call my office and leave a message with my secretary."

"O.K. Doc, but am I going crazy?" Mr. Canton asked.

"I don't think so, I just think you have a very vivid imagination," Ronaw stated calmly. "Besides, last time I saw you, I do not remember a third eye, so I think you are okay."

Mr. Canton laughed curtly at Ronaw's attempt at humor and replied, "You know what

Doc? You're right, I don't know what would cause such a strange dream."

Reassuringly Ronaw replied, "Well, let me ponder on what you just expressed to see if I can find some rationale behind the imagery and I will get back to you in a few days, O.K.?"

"Sure Doc, have a good day." Mr. Canton said as he hung up.

Ronaw thought to himself, "That was the weirdest dream sequence yet by any of my clients." He couldn't just shuck it off like a wild story that the mind could generally come up with. Something about it got under his skin and festered like a blister. He just couldn't figure out what it was.

Adair Rowan

Chapter 6

Somewhere in the remote, southern, Cumberland Plateau area of Tennessee, there was a facility. Within that facility, there was a cold dark room. The only light within this room came from an advanced computer control station that covered three-fourths of that room. The highly sensitive technology in this room was on loan from the IDF1 black-ops branch of the Pentagon.

The organization was like an underworld formed by the top military minds of the world. This computer station was monitored by three shifts, of six individuals per shift. They were all disciplined in various arts of self-defense. All were registered as lethal weapons by the government and trained in guerrilla warfare; they could break down firearms like a pack of chewing gum. Many of them had been labeled as heartless.

The mission was their reason for being. They all sat, quietly, their breathing barely audible. Their glares were intense and piercing. Watching, waiting, staring. Their faces showed no tension, looking like statues carved in stone. They watched the panels silently. They knew that if something on those panels blinked the wrong color, all hell would break loose. There was no joking or smiling in this room.

There were two radar-tracking systems, which displayed 3D images of the solar system in real time. The images were created from the information transmitted by several hundred satellites. There was a blip that they'd all been tracking. The blip seemed to flash into existence one week ago and began moving on an erratic course toward the sun.

At first, it was thought to be a small meteorite that had traversed the darkness between the galaxies and found itself finally being tugged about by the various gravitational fields of the outer planets, moons, and debris in the far orbits of our solar system. This assumption was quickly laid to rest as the object passed several different planets and altered its course dramatically.

It even seemed to split into two separate parts during its journey. The object slowly continued its various course changes until finally entered a parked orbit several thousand miles above the Earths equator. It remained there for a few days seemingly dormant.

Two monitors displayed the hemispheres of Earth. One monitor showed the northern half and the other the southern half. As the object finally moved and the other monitoring system showed it's projected heading, the monitors of the other two monitors zoomed in and tracked the object through the upper atmosphere as it descended slowly.

The object didn't seem to fall like a

meteorite or other known debris that left a trail in the atmosphere. It almost didn't leave much of a disturbance in the air at all. It was like a ghost you could see that had no effect on its surroundings. The monitors continued to zoom in until they both showed the outline for the state of Georgia. As the object continued its descent, it flew over the state of Georgia until and entered the airspace above Tennessee.

A few moments later one of the other monitors flashed red off and on indicating probable impact in the displayed vicinity. The men stared at the computers a little longer to make sure it wasn't going to change into the standard dull blue screen that indicated all was clear. They waited one minute... two minutes... three minutes...

In the center of the room, an ebony hand reached out of a cloak of all-encompassing darkness and rested upon the emergency red security digi-phone. There was only one button on this phone. The dark hand waited. Four minutes passed as he lifted the receiver off the mount... Five minutes; the screens flickered, then displayed the following message:

```
-OBJECTS OBSERVED...
COMPOSITION:          PREVIOUSLY
CONFIRMED MATERIALS...
ORIGIN:           NON-TERRESTRIAL
SATELLITE TYPE #XK13...
INSTRUCTIONS:
```
IMPLEMENT ORDER---□□□□

```
DEF:        TRACK-SUBDUE-ACQUIRE-
RETRIEVE
FURTIVE ACTION REQUIRED
COMMENCE              PREPARATION
PROCEDURE
CODE: TRNSFG-7
```

The dark ebony hand placed the receiver back onto the base in one smooth motion. The room remained silent except for the soft humming sound that the computers were generating, and the sound of the processing unit as it forced cool air through the ventilation shafts that were mounted above and below the various terminals.

If one strained to listen, one could almost hear the slow, timed breathing of each person manning their assigned areas of equipment.

The primary monitor located on the back wall of the room glowed fluorescent orange along with a sharp emergency ready tone. Everyone within the room turned to observe the screen. They rose from their seats and stood at attention as they read ...

```
MISSION: LOCATE
CONTAIN
RETRIEVE
NO LEAKAGE
TOP PRIORITY
CODE LEVEL P/CNC
END MESSAGE
```

After a few moments a strong and unwavering

voice issued the final command.

ASSEMBLE.

Adair Rowan

Chapter 7

In the marshlands deep in the forested swamp of Tennessee, IT fell. In reality, IT didn't fall, IT glided; swimming through the air like a fish through water, floating like a feather on air currents. IT was oval in shape and had a dark, oily texture. IT was completely smooth except for the underbelly, which had several bilaterally placed obtrusions around its base. It was clearly unnatural in its current surroundings. All manner of animal turned tail and ran in the opposite direction. The insects stopped flying as if frozen in fear. The birds stopped singing. The fish swam to the bottom of the marsh looking for rocks to hide beneath. IT was definitely emitting a dangerous aura.

The obtrusions had a soft glow about them as the object shifted its equator so that it would be perfectly perpendicular to the water above, which it now hovered. The slimmer pole of IT was pointed north leaving the bulkier pole pointed south. IT made no sound with this maneuver. It was as if time had stopped for everything but IT. No rustling of leaves by lizards on branches, no movement within the water causing it to ripple by some unseen but ever-present amphibious creature

The object began to ripple like the surface of a pond struck by a pebble. The rippling started at the slim end and continued on toward the bulkier end and back. IT hovered about fifteen feet off the ground for about an hour without any outward motion, now it was rippling. The ripples sped up, as out of the surrounding stillness came the roar of a hover boat fan. And as the sound got closer, the object lowered itself onto the murky marsh waters. When its underbelly struck the surface, it curved from the middle outward to resemble the underbelly of a speedboat.

"YAAAAHHOOOO!" A young man yelled from beyond the embankments cover of trees.
IT was halfway submerged by the time the hover-boat was within visual range. The driver of the hovercraft turned and steered directly for IT. Lionel was his name, and he was considered the town idiot. He was mentally challenged but was more than able to take care of himself in the swamps and marshlands in which he had grown up.

As he cleared the bend, he almost ran dead smack into a mound. He diverted his course reflexively, just wide enough to avoid a collision, then circled around it a few times trying to determine what it was. At first, he thought . . .
"Another mound of "greasy earth that the prospectors were always interested in,"
But there was something different about this mound of "greasy earth" It looked too smooth. Being curious about anything new in his swamp,

he decided to get close enough to touch the stuff. He pulled his craft close enough to touch the thing. He reached out a hand cautiously, wondering what the others would do if they were here. His fingertips touched its surface. It felt like "a.... big.... tomato."

Cautiously, he decided to touch it again. As he reached out to touch IT again, IT reached out and took hold of him. IT extended layers of its surface, like an amoeba, and pulled him within IT. He let out a few strained grunts and moans, but it happened so fast. Before his mind could actually understand, his body realized that he was no longer outside. He was inside the thing. It felt like "JELLO," only a lot thicker. He tried to cry out, only to realize that he couldn't.

"Am I dead?" he wondered.

He had no experience with that so he couldn't believe that. Then he felt something brush up against him. Unable to turn to see what it was terrified him. Shivering in fear, he tried his best to look around. Whatever this was, it was very murky. He could see movement along the edges of his vision. Whatever was moving was getting closer to him. He didn't like that. Then he felt a sharp pain in his hand. It felt like a nail being jabbed through his palm. Then there was a numb grinding along his wrist. He turned to look but could see only a vague outline. He tried to shake it loose but found that with each motion the pain grew worse. The pain struck in his foot next, right below the ankle, and progressively got worse as it rose up his leg to his thigh.

There was a bit of dim light filtering through the goo from the sky above. He looked down to where the pain was coming from and gazed upon a dozen eyes, which were strewn across the head structure of whatever this thing was. It was working its way up his body. The shock of what he was seeing was too much to handle. Something so alien, incomprehensible, it was eating him alive. He was alive, but he wasn't breathing.

"How is this possible?" Even with a mind as simple as his, there were questions about the possibility of his current dilemma. The pain receptors in his brain were overloaded as the creatures chewed their way through his pelvic region. He looked away from the advancing death that gnawed him toward oblivion and into the face of something more hideous than his fragile mind and limited vocabulary would allow him to define. One went for his other hand and he felt the pressure, then the sharpness of what he could only conclude was teeth. More eyes, teeth, sharp appendages, and spiny limbs were advancing upward. He wanted to scream and tried but the goo filled his mouth and he could not. He wanted to cry, but he could not do that either. All he could do was fill the striated bellies of these creatures that found him to be a tasty morsel.

The pain went on so long until his mind cut off the reception, no longer acknowledging the sparks. He could hear the muffled crunch of his bones resounding within the gel.

The creatures were relentless. They moved like an electric carving knife, cutting, slashing, and grinding his bones. At that moment, Lionel realized that there would be nothing left of him.

Crunch!! One was up to his shoulder and appeared to be still hungry unless of course, he was only a light snack for these things of which all he could see were semi-glossy, glowing, red eyes.

"Yes; darkness and numbness." He thought.

The darkness around the edges of his field of vision was increasing in size. He no longer felt the pain. He thought to himself, "So this is what shock feels like."

He no longer had a heartbeat or rather, one that he could identify as his own. He saw another head. It was above him. It moved closer to his head, its mouth moving like a mulching machine on a low setting. Those horrible jaws opened wide. He couldn't believe the clarity of his mind within these final moments of his life. It wasn't like the mouth of a dog or an alligator, nor any other beast that had ever been known first hand by mankind.

There were two writhing, squirming tongues within a four-sided mouth, with each side appearing to be solid. They encompassed more teeth than he could begin to count. The upper section contained five long translucent incisors that could, from appearance, pierce the skull of a man with the slightest pressure. The lower section had six of these incisors and two openings, one on each side. He had no clue of its purpose.

The thing closed its jaws, covering his eyes, and darkness completely engulfed him. He heard his skull as it began to crack and splinter under the pressure of the unearthly jaws. He felt nothing but terror as his mind was invaded by a sickening and repulsive consciousness.

Upon realizing what was happening to him, the revelation of these creatures' intent and purpose was also made clear to him. He fought to keep control of his own thoughts but felt them slipping out of his grasp.

"My, gasp... Ha! What a concept" were the last human thoughts that flowed through his mind before he was no longer...

The mound expanded and bulged from beneath the marsh a quarter of an inch more than it had been before the digestion of Lionel Hansen. The mound began to head northwards in the swamp toward the wooded area, the direction from which Lionel had come.

IT was no longer just a mound either; it was now a hive of anxious creatures, waiting to inflict the severity of its hunger upon those who had escaped their grasp. IT knew no concept of time until it's ingestion of Lionel.

IT recognized that from its descent through the atmosphere of this place called Earth, someone, somewhere, had been tracking it. IT knew it had to move again, but at this time it needed a moment to rest and calm the others within.

Adair Rowan

Chapter 8

The Squad was fully equipped and operating at alert status in less than fifteen minutes. During practice runs, they had usually taken twenty minutes to be fully equipped and all enlisted personnel accounted for and ready for briefing. All eighteen members were rigidly sitting in the briefing forum, on carpeted oversized steps that had been commandeered solely for this conference. They had been prepared by years of training. Reconnaissance missions, self-discipline and self-sacrifice were requirements. They were ready to face anything known to man with a stern chin and balls of steel, but no one had a clue on the topic of what they were up against.

Clip, clop, clip, clop, was the sound that everyone waiting heard. The sound of hard-soled military issue boots drew closer to the forum doorway. He was on his way. All eyes were on the doorknob, which jiggled a little then slowly, turned over halfway as the doors locking mechanism gave entrance to the legend on the other side. The door moved, and the man who entered was the embodiment of strength. An imposing 6-foot 6-inch ebony figure, he snapped a quick salute, with his left hand and headed straight for the podium.

There were murmurs through the crowd as he moved, and they recognized him. "Commander!" each soldier saluted in sequence as he passed by. He did not wait for the occupants of the room to salute in return. His broad hands held a file, which was almost as thick as a Stephen King novel. His uniform was snug, and his shoes reflected the rooms yellow light like flashes from a multitude of cameras as he walked. He had massive arms and shoulders. His eyes were coal black and clear, like those of an owl scanning the darkness for the slightest movement of its prey. He was clean-shaven, but his face still had the rugged, tough appearance of an outdoorsman. His quick rise and extreme prejudice methodology when dealing with problems earned him the reputation of a man to be reckoned with.

Commander Edwards stood behind the podium, looking out into all the excited, eager, and a few confused faces in his crew. They were all focused on him with an intense glare. He clicked on the microphone. The room was so quiet that you could almost hear the Commanders heartbeat even though he stood approximately a foot and a half from the microphone. It drummed along slowly, but strongly.

He began in a strong, steady voice, "You are the elite, that this country has to offer. You are probably wondering why you are here and what all this means. I'll get straight to it. I handpicked each and every one of you from a list of over twenty-eight thousand soldiers from coast to coast, to be a part of this squad. You have what it takes, in my opinion, to handle things that no one, other than you can. You are beyond the normal people society in many ways. Your intelligence and genetics played a huge part in your selection as well. Throughout this program, your stamina, guts and determination, made you the perfect candidates for this situation. You have all been here within this facility, for the past year, babysitting computer monitors for a good reason. I know that it's been difficult not to get bored, but your attention to detail is why I also singled each of you out. I know you're curious, so I must tell you, now is the time for action. The drills and combat training you've been so diligently performing are only the tip of the iceberg in comparison to what you may experience during our mission."

"What you have been keeping watch over is the Quad -S defense data matrix, or the Solar Surveillance Satellite System. This has been online for a little more than the last twenty years. It was approved first by President Clinton and reapproved by President Obama for surveillance of and non-disclosure of UFO activity. This program became black budget, Need-to-know Zeta Level clearance only once Obama left office, and therefore our current president is unaware of its existence. Many in Washington thought it was a waste of taxpaying dollars, but for certain bills to escape veto, they approved this two billion dollar a year program that enables us to detect and observe anything which is of Earthly or non-Earthly origin that enters our solar system. Over twenty years ago since the program was launched, it has been, in effect, the guardian of human existence here on Earth.

The network includes over two thousand eighty satellites strategically placed throughout the solar system. Each is independent but collectively linked to one another to form a spatial grid. The computers you monitor are the secondary brain of the whole network. As you are aware, the UKNI orbital satellite system processes all the information and verifies what we see on a separate network link. This network identifies each object within the grid, extrapolates size parameters, gravitational ratios, space radiation, composition, speed and trajectory of any and all objects in our solar system that could be of any type of benefit or threat.

When the network was first put online and became fully functional, there was an object which could not be identified (with then existing information), which seemed to be exiting our solar system at unheard of velocities."

Every set of eyes in the room was still upon him as he continued.

"Upon my appointment to this assignment, I began to follow up on the information stored in the program's archives. I followed the trajectory of the object closely and it's increase in velocity to see if I could pinpoint, at least to a degree; a probable destination. I made an educated guess and concluded that the particular area of space into which it was headed contained nothing at that time. This didn't make much sense at first because there had to be some form of intelligence guiding the object, so I began to add different variables to my calculations. With respect to universal expansion momentum, I have reason to believe that the destination of the object is a galaxy known now as Messier 51 or M51."

Clearing his throat, Edwards continued. "This was a reasonable conclusion because the departure of the object was only about five light years off course. Given its maneuverability, obvious intelligence and unknown method of propulsion, which defied the laws of physics, I figured that they aimed their vessel where that particular galaxy would be upon the end of the five light year travel period. Understand that information about this galaxy has been shrouded in mystery due to gaseous anomalies and the discovery of dense clouds of dark matter. I could only theorize a vague guess upon their intended destination within that galaxy."

"This particular galaxy is similar to the Milky Way to the naked eye. Although it appears the same, upon closer examination, it seems that there is one major difference. One of its spiral arm extensions has a region that looks like a smaller galaxy is growing out of it."

He gave his last statement a chance to sink in, which was accompanied by a few intrigued grunts and astonished moans.

"The composition of the object which left our solar system was beyond our scientific understanding."

"Excuse me, sir," a brisk young officer interrupted.

Ignoring the interruption, Edwards continued,

"The composition of the object was carbonous, but it contained a substantial amount of a polymorphic material which was enclosed within some type of metallic substance which has only been found by extensive satellite scrutiny, in two places on Earth."

A burly, redheaded young officer stood and asked, "Sir, where exactly are these locations?"

Edwards took a moment and seemed to think about the question. As silence crept across the room, He glared at the young officer and in a booming voice, he spoke.

"Young man, if I took time to address every question we would be stuck in briefing for the next year. Right now, I need everyone to simply listen during this briefing"

Edwards glared at the young officer, and the young man quickly sat down with a grimace while the rest of the officers snickered quietly to themselves.

Edwards continued, "A large deposit of the substance has been located just off the coastal area of Florida, in the form of some type of casing. What was in the casing has yet to be determined, but that is a job to be done by the lab boys."

He hit a few keys on the terminal mounted on the podium and lights went dim. A projection of Florida appeared on the HD monitor. A few indeterminate murmurs escaped the crew, but nothing else was said.

"Within the five-hundred-mile marker which expands from the farthest shores of the island of Bermuda is the exact location. Now, approximately ten or fifteen miles out is another island. This island does not appear on any normal map that you can purchase at a local fuel pump or supermarket. Its existence has only come to light recently through absence extrapolation. Basically, the whole island emits some type of disruptive field that obstructs its appearance on all previously known electronic mapping scans. This island has the largest concentration of whatever this material is which matched compositionally, the shell of the aforementioned object. There are however small concentrations of this same material located along the southeastern Tennessee marsh areas of the U.S. This is the reason why we've only been monitoring two states."

The men and women of the Squad mumbled for a few moments as the lights came back on and silence quickly gripped the room leaving it eerie, like a mausoleum just before midnight. The Commander looked out across the podium as if he was looking into the very souls of the members seated in that room and said,

"What is currently happening is something, we hoped never would, but we prepared for. An object was identified on a course trajectory that indicated its final destination as Earth. It matched the previous description of twenty years ago only this time it was exactly twice the aforementioned objects size. When I say this, I don't mean to give or take a few inches or even centimeters I mean exactly. What was odd while monitoring this object, was that as the object reached Jupiter's gravitational envelope, it split into two distinct units. One of them is the object that crossed our monitoring stations in Georgia and Tennessee, however the other, we have reason to believe was drawn into the atmosphere of Jupiter and was crushed. This hasn't been verified but due to no evidence to the contrary and what we know of Jupiter's atmosphere; that has been the conclusion thus far.

Ladies and gentlemen, we have an extreme situation happening and judging from the swiftness at which it is developing, I must provide you with the equipment that you will need."

Chapter 9

Southeastern Tennessee was not aware of the extenuating circumstances that were at work in its marshes. Alongside a six-mile stretch of Hwy 61, ran a fifty-foot deep creek that rustled beside it in plain view. The creek was full of weeds, mud, bugs, fish and all the other typical things within your basic creek. On this warm sunny day; however, it also held something in its slow-moving gullet that just wasn't normal.

A hermit who lived in the marshlands of southeastern Tennessee used the creek to supply his supper a lot. He knew how filthy the water was but didn't care. He also knew that it was just a matter of time before his luck ran out and something he ate would possibly kill him. He lay along the embankment with his burgundy and gold sleeping bag nestled comfortably beneath his head, with his legs sprawled out. A fishing pole stabbed half a handle deep into the earth for support was his focus right now. He watched and waited for that tugging and whirring to start, which would indicate that he had caught his dinner. He had been there for almost two hours now and hadn't caught a thing. This seemed odd to him because usually it only took about half-an-hour before he caught something.

Meanwhile, the hive eased its way out of the swamp to the creek-bed. It followed the weak current, which moved only about eight miles an hour. The hive was restless, the cry of hunger of its twenty or so inhabitants writhed like the anxious little children. During the first five miles, all that the hive had fed on were the small fish and frogs that had the misfortune of swimming along the path the hive followed. The fish weren't even befitting of the title of a light snack in comparison to the hive's hunger.

Lying there on the embankment the hermit had the time to think about all that had happened in his life. He had lived a simple life, with few complications as of late. He was normal by any standards. Once known as Officer Antione Druman, he was a local cop in the nearby town of GLEN ALICE, until he had to shoot down one of the neighbor's children. The teenager had taken up refuge in a small wooden home about three miles outside of town. Before doing so, he had led the police on a high-speed chase on back roads and country lanes. He broke into an elderly lady's home and killed her.

Hiding in her home, he defied the multiple requests from the local police department to come out with his hands in the air. Instead of relinquishing his weapon, he came out with his gun blazing. Officers ducked for cover behind their cars as bullets whizzed by. Some officers took pot shots at the offender but missed because they were ducking at the same time. Antione took one carefully aimed shot at the young man's chest. That one shot ended not only the kid's life but also, Antione's desire to continue as a policeman. He'd been living off the land for over ten years now. He knew the area, which was about thirty miles in diameter, like the back of his crusty, dusty hands. His thoughts slowly turned to dreams as he succumbed to the weariness that a ten-mile walk in 105-degree weather would force on anyone.

The mound glided through the water silently, as if part of the water. Then something touched it. Something so small and insignificant, but this small thing grabbed hold and wouldn't let go. A small area of the mound became transparent as a colony of eyes examined the afflicted region. It was barely noticeable by human standards, but the eyes that examined this area weren't human by any means. They had acquired the capacity for human thought, thanks to their ingestion of Lionel. The only problem was that the thoughts of this Lionel were far from clear, in fact, they were sort of random with a lot of discontinuity. The object that had snagged the hive was called a fishhook, which meant there was a person nearby. The top of the hive became transparent as multiple eyes began to scan the embankment with intense anxiety and desire. The embankment was littered with cans, paper cups, tires, hamburger wrappers and such. Then the eyes gazed upon a man sprawled upon the sandy embankment. The mound stopped moving which caused ripples within the water and had to change course in order to continue to where it was going. The man arose slowly, apparently alerted by the noise from the fishing rod. It looked as if he was alone. He looked to see if his hook was caught on something. By this time the hive had dropped just below the surface of the creek. The man saw nothing, so he returned to his padding on the embankment and closed his eyes.

Antoine's gut was telling him that something was wrong, but he was so tired, and he wanted to go to sleep. He decided to take another look around before nodding off. He scanned the creek again and his eyes settled on a mound of jelly looking stuff. It was smooth on the top and was apparently still in the water. There was something odd about it. He noticed how it wasn't moving, but it seemed like it was holding everything still. He'd seen all types of sedimentary mounds that the creeks in this area had accumulated and had never seen one quite like this. It was too smooth to be mud and sand like most of the ones he'd seen. It wasn't being slowly stripped away by the passing current either. He moved toward his fishing pole and cut the line loose. The mound still did not continue downstream. Maybe it was stuck on something. He thought about it for a minute and decided that whatever it was stuck on wasn't all that important to him. He slowly rolled up the sleeping bag and nonchalantly tied it up to his backpack that was lying next to where he had been dozing off. Out of the corner of his eye, he saw that the mound was closer. It was moving slowly, but even from the distance of twenty or thirty feet, he could still see its motion.

He strapped on the backpack and reached behind his back, underneath the thin, dingy, windbreaker he was wearing to feel the reassuring blue steel of his Magnum 357, which he kept when he turned in his badge. The mound was slowly rising out of the water. He could hear the water droplets pat the sand. He started off, at a slow walk, toward the nearest cluster of trees that was several yards away. At first, he didn't run. Antione was a bit curious; he wondered what this thing was. Actually, it was downright bugging the hell out of him. He looked back and noted that the mound was entirely out of the water now, but it wasn't moving. He did, however, recognize that the surface facing him began to bulge and quiver as if something within it was trying to break through. Antione upped his pace to a trot toward the trees. He glanced back and saw what he could only think of as legs touching the ground. Antione really began to pick up the pace. What he saw was creepy. The many pairs of legs that made him think of a giant spider. His heart began to beat faster, the adrenaline was flooding his system in a fight or flight response to the perception of this potential threat. The torso of the creature was emerging. It vaguely resembled something that he had seen before. He couldn't quite place his finger on it though, and at this point, he really didn't care. He just wanted to be somewhere else. Where, didn't really matter, just anyplace but there at that moment, observing what he was seeing. Hopefully, he could make it to the shelter of the trees and have time then, to figure out what it was.

There was a noise behind him that sounded like the engine of an industrial lawn mower. He looked back to where he had last seen the mound and its spawn only to find that the creature was no longer behind him. He also knew, however, that whatever it was, hadn't gone far. He stopped and looked around carefully, left, right, behind him. Finally, he turned back toward the trees and realized that he should've just continued, without stopping, toward the trees. He heard the noise but couldn't get a bearing on its direction. The thought occurred to look up. As he did so, the jaws of the creature were coming for his face. With all the speed and agility he could muster, he fell back and rolled away from it. He dropped the backpack during his roll and pulled the revolver in one swift, precise motion. As he arose from his maneuver, he simultaneously began to pull the trigger. A wail of unknown caliber escaped the creature's mighty jaws. It vibrated the air for miles around.

In Dayton, a store owner who was taking out the garbage heard it and spilled half the trash out of the bag. He cursed himself for being so jumpy. He'd been having this odd feeling all afternoon and didn't know why. A waitress named Sheila at the local outdoor Pub-N-Grub almost spilled a tray loaded with glasses of pop and juice on a group of teenagers who were waiting for their burgers. A group of old men sitting outside playing dominoes heard it too. One of the old men was about to pitch his domino toward the playing table, and the noise startled him so that he flung it past the formation and broke the glass of water sitting in front of the gentleman sitting across from him. They both glanced around wondering about the sound but eventually settled back into their game. All of the people in the northeastern half of town heard the sound, but no one had a clue as to what it was.

The creature fell back from the impact mercury tipped lead dumdums. Druman dived behind a nearby boulder for cover. The noise had stopped and the creature was apparently examining itself. He took aim at what seemed to be the head of the creature and repeatedly pulled the trigger until it just clicked in response. The creature fell backward and squirmed on the ground. Antione knew that he wasn't out the woods. Springing up from the ground he began to sprint at a brisk pace through the forest towards the nearest sheriff's station; three miles south of his location, just outside of Dayton along Route 27. He could get hold of a radio and send a warning to the town and get help from the military if necessary.

He ran through the woods with the ease of a panther. His thoughts raced as quickly as the thumping of his heart did in his ears. He couldn't believe what he had just seen, and at the same time, he couldn't believe that the gunshot, even that from a 357 Magnum, did not stop it.

He heard the creature's cry again. It wasn't very far away. The sound was somewhat muffled. He had to be careful. It could fly and he couldn't, so he chose to stay within the thickly wooded areas. He slowed his run down to a steady jog to conserve energy. It should only take him about fifteen minutes to reach the security station if the creature didn't reach him first.

The creature slowly and somewhat awkwardly rose to a standing position. It was stunned but not severely injured. There was a deep gash that extended about two and a half inches into what could be described as its head, where the first few bullets hit. The other shots missed. A few eyes were damaged, but there were a dozen or so others that would compensate for that. The tingling sensation of its regenerative process signaled that the healing had begun. It knew that it's damaged eyes could not be regenerated. The place where the bullets caused damage would callous over in a few moments. That area would be harder to rupture, but the sockets would stay an open wound, until its death. According to the new concept of time it had been introduced to, that roughly came to about three to four centuries.

Sometime later the sheriff was just walking out of the station when he noticed someone emerging from the woods. He did not recognize him initially, even up close. What he did see was the dark object in the hand of the man. He saw that the man was, in fact, reloading a weapon. The sheriff put his hand on his gun and dropped behind the nearest squad car. He heard a familiar voice that was out of breath.

"Sheriff Jordan!" The man yelled from a distance.

Jordan could tell that the man was still winded.

"Antione?" he yelled.

He saw the head of the man nod in response, but he kept his pistol un-strapped. As Antoine got closer, the sheriff could see the agitated expression on his face.

"What's the problem, Antione?"

Antione staggered up to him, out of breath and mumbling something in a low raspy voice as he re-holstered his weapon.

"Monster, big insect, spider-like, ...No like a Praying Mantis, No, well yeah. It is like the product of a Mantis and a Spider mated. It had six to eight legs; huge head, teeth, whole bunch eyes.

Jordan looked at Antione with confusion. "What are you talking about? You're not speaking coherently."

"I saw it, Sheriff," he said as he caught his breath.

"Saw what?"

"This thing, Sheriff, it came up out of the creek along route 27. I was fishing and I saw it."

"Wait a minute Antione. Come on in and calm down."

"No, there's no time Sheriff. You got to warn the town, call the Army, the Marines, get some guns, grenades, bazookas or something."

Jordan just stared at Antione for a moment trying to figure out if lying about in the elements had finally affected his brain.

"Calm down Antione!"

Antione stopped talking for a moment and looked at Jordan's face.

"Slow down and tell me exactly what happened."

"Jordan, I was laying on the embankment of the creek along route 27, doing my normal fishing, and I didn't catch no fish. I wondered why, but I just figured it was a slow day. Then my hook caught on something and I got up. When I looked to see what I'd caught, I was a bit surprised. It was this big shiny black mound, kind of shaped like a football. It started rising up out of the water, so I headed toward the forest, real slow like. Then I heard this sound like a balloon being twisted into an animal shape, you know, like at kids parties. I looked around and saw a whole bunch of legs coming out of the thing; I know that it wasn't normal because the mound was floating about six feet above the ground. I watched the legs contact the ground and a torso, head and other appendages of some kind of monster came out of the thing too."

"How big was this black mound or whatever it was?" Jordan asked as he leaned in.

"It was maybe about thirty feet in length and about fifteen feet wide I reckon."

"So what happened next?"

"I turned and took a few steps toward the forest then looked behind me to see what was going on. The creature wasn't there though. I looked around and didn't see a thing. I looked up and saw the jaws of this thing coming at my head. I fell back and fired my Magnum into its skull; I guess that was its skull. It made this God-awful noise and I shot it again. I took off into the forest and prayed I'd make it to your post in one piece."

"Have you been drinking Antione?"

"I don't even have enough money to buy liquor Jordan, and, I gave that up a while back man, you know that."

"Are you sure about what you saw?"

"As sure as I was... when I had to shoot that kid, Sheriff."

His words lingered.

Jordan walked back and forth across the room for a few minutes.

"Look, I know it doesn't sound real, but I'm telling you we do not have time to question what I saw."

Just as Antione finished his sentence, there was a growing noise from outside.

"Uh! Sheriff."

"What is it, Antione?"

"Is anyone cutting the grass nearby?"

"Not that I know of, most people don't bother with cutting the grass all the way out here, they just let the local wildlife have at it. Why?"

"Cause either someone's cutting grass, or we've got company, and if we've got company we're in deep crap!"

Jordan saw the wild look in Antione's eyes and figured that either he was delusional or whatever it was he had experienced had scared him half to death. Banking on the latter, Sheriff Jordan pulled his service weapon from his shoulder harness and checked the clip. Fully loaded he ran toward the nearest door, but before he could reach it, the wall cracked inward. It puckered and some small fragments of drywall flew across the room as something slammed into it from the outside. Jordan was taken by surprise and tripped over the leg of a chair. Luckily he had good reflexes, so instead of breaking his ankle he merely allowed his body to go slightly limp as he fell forward into a front roll and back up to his feet barely losing any momentum, dropping his sidearm in the motion. He reached back for his gun as the wall exploded and chunks of wood and plaster flew across the room. Antione pulled the table down on its side and took cover. The sheriff covered his face so that he wouldn't be struck in the face by any of the flying debris. A smooth, graceful four-fingered hand reached in and grabbed hold of the wall and pulled it outward. The sheriff took notice and dove for the nearest desk for some cover until he could get a better look. He heard what sounded like an enormous lawnmower and couldn't believe what he saw as he peeked over the top of the desk. The creature was hovering about two feet off the ground. It was huge, about seven feet tall. The wings on its back were moving at such a velocity that they were nothing but a wide blur making it difficult to judge their size. The sheriff saw Antione pull his Magnum and take aim.

"No, Antione, don't shoot!" Jordan shouted,

The sheriffs' warning was too late. The creature, now alerted of the sheriff's position by his outburst, moved towards him. Antione pulled the trigger. The projectile hit between its upper wings and the creature fell hard to the ground but managed to land on its legs. The room was silent but for a moment before being filled with the creatures ghastly wailing. The sheriff was staring in disbelief as the monster reached around and felt for the wounded area. The hand, when brought back, was covered with a fluorescent orange jelly-like liquid. It looked at the sheriff with some of its eyes. The eyes seemed to emit a slight glow, even visible in broad daylight. It stopped moving. The four-parted mouth opened to reveal a horizontal row of razor-sharp teeth. The Sheriff didn't take time to study the creature any more: he reached behind his back for the extra clip of dumdums, loaded the clip and emptied it in the direction of the creature's head. There was a short wail that escaped the creature as the dumdums hammered into its exoskeleton. Two of the eight rounds broke through and came to reside just inside of the cool but firm tissue of the creature's entrails. The sheriff stared at the creature as it fell to the ground.

He called to Antione. "Hey! Let's get the hell out of here and call for some help."

As they were departing down a hallway opposite where the creature had entered the room, they saw that the creature was starting to move again. The sheriff pulled his keys and unlocked a closet outside of the room they had just exited. He opened it up to reveal a wall of weaponry. He grabbed an A.P.50, military ordinance, with a compact grenade launcher, laser sighting, and titanium piercing rounds. Jordan tossed one to Antione asking, "Think you can handle this little baby here?"

Antione stared at the weapon and said, "Hell, I don't know, but I learn quickly."

Jordan grabbed a can of ammo and reached for an AP50 of his own. They took off down the hallway. Behind them, they could hear the creature. It was on its feet now, moving slowly, but still in pursuit.

They made it out of the door and halfway to the car before they saw another one perched on a thick tree branch about seventy or so feet away. It was just spreading its wings when Antione took aim and pulled the trigger. He felt the recoil, as it slammed hard against his shoulder. He heard a hollow popping sound and the monster grabbed at what appeared to be its neck. Antione meant to shoot it with the rounds but had accidentally hit it with a grenade.

The creature took flight, and then suddenly, it flopped to the ground as it's shoulder burst into flames, then the nearest arm, the neck, and finally the head. It stopped moving. The remains popped and crackled with fire. The sheriff jumped into the car and started it. He revved the engine as he waited for Antione to get in. The creature's body was in the middle of the lot's entrance blocking their exit. They put on their seatbelts; the sheriff threw the car in gear and punched the accelerator.

The vehicle hit the creature's body and bucked a little, but continued through the flaming carcass. The limbs and lower body of the creature fell to the ground with a rubbery thud. They didn't stop to check on the creature's condition; instead, they sped off toward the nearest road and headed for town. Jordan clicked on the cars radio transmitter and began to tune to the emergency all broadcast band.

Adair Rowan

Chapter 10

Preparations were being made deep inside an underground; top-secret, military installation. Commander Edwards was once again briefing his team. This time it was about the armaments constructed specifically for an unknown adversary.

"The basic uniform for infantry, which you've grown accustomed to, we feel can't and won't offer enough protection. Since we are uncertain about what it is that we may encounter, we have designed new, more advanced, combat gear that must always be worn during this operation. That is, whether or not you are inside or outside of the prototype vehicles you will be traveling in."

A young woman in her mid-twenties rose from her seat with a salute toward Edwards, and said in a stern but respectful tone, "Combat gear, why do we need combat gear if our main objective is to capture and contain?"

"Good question. The reason is that during the few months that preceded the departure of the first object from our then, unprepared defenses, reports of unexplained, as well as unconventional viciousness were intercepted from the Georgia and Tennessee areas. Extensive file records contain lists of mutilations, and terrible cases of dismemberment filled shelves and cabinets in many of the counties' morgues. The only reason that mass panic didn't break out was due to a government cover-up."

Stepping from around the podium he opened the folder and passed around a copy of one of the files. As the members of this elite team passed around the folder and looked at the photos, there were a lot of raised eyebrows throughout the room. During all this, Edwards kept a serious, grim look on his face.

"I believe in preparing my people with everything available to me. I want you to know what I know, and since I'm going into this with you I felt that you all should know that we are facing something so far beyond what we've ever experienced, we can only hope that the advanced weaponry and body armor will help us stop what could possibly turn into an invasion."

"An invasion sir . . ."

"That's exactly what our head advisors believe. Based on the premise that these objects are composed of the same previously unknown elements and construction, they believe that this could simply be this races equivalence to a scouting team."

The air in the room seemed to become stale during the few moments Edwards took to allow his words to sink in. The members stared back and forth in bewilderment, and some even looked apprehensive. Edwards took those few moments to collect his thoughts and continue with the briefing.

"Now, our scientific minds have been working on several different prototypes of body armor over the years. Through the various methods of testing, they finally narrowed down the group to one all-purpose, durable and adaptive model. The new uniforms have been under top-secret production for the last year. They are designed for a snug fit. They will provide the maximum support for your back arms and legs. There are thirty-eight suits, two for each individual. The suits are composed of a lightweight, but solid, Titanium-Admantium, sentient symbiotic alloy that has been provided through classified channels. Within the suit are bio-monitoring units as well as bio-amplifying augmenters. Once activated, your speed and strength will increase exponentially. The helmets, with which I personally have been involved, are designed to interact directly with the miniature psyionic emitters that have been placed within your brains."

"The question that many of you may have is; what effect will these transmitters have on your bodies. They have been tested for every known and even some very far-fetched predicaments, allergic reactions and all, and have passed every test with flying colors. The reason they have is that they are bio-emitters, which naturally occur within the human body. The only difference is that your bodies have been hormonally enhanced, making them more pronounced and therefore more powerful so that they can be read and responded to by the highly sensitive equipment that you will be wearing. Don't misunderstand people; I too have been altered just as you have. I wouldn't subject anyone under my command to something I'm not willing to be subjected to. As I was saying, the helmets are also constructed of the TAS3 alloy. The inside of the helmets are coated with a bio-reactant industrial gel which will conform to your cranial structure, so I suggest that you don't try to yank off your helmet unless you are trying to take off your head along with it. The emitters in your brain also interface with the gel in your helmets. At first, it will seem odd, but we begin training in the suits in exactly forty-eight hours, so I suggest that you call your loved ones, and get your affairs in order. Duty starts in exactly forty-eight hours from now, see you all then. That is all; dismissed!"

He saluted the soldiers and shook each hand. It was not required by duty, but he was compelled to look each of the members in the eye for reassurance. He could not help wondering whether or not he, or any of his Squad, would make it through the upcoming mission.

Chapter 11

Touch down for Ronaw's flight was at around twelve noon. Mr. Lakur's extended land cruiser with a driver awaited just off the runway and was used to transport him to the Lakur property.

Arriving on the grounds of the Lakur retreat was a breathtaking experience for Ronaw. Centered on the grounds was a twelve-roomed mini-mansion. Its curvature and sweeping columns projected comfort to the mind. It was a split-level home with an intricately etched, translucent dome. From a distance, Ronaw could see that the dome was an enclosed observatory.

There were two humongous statues of stalking black pumas, which stood about twelve feet in height and dwarfed the front doors of the home. The doors were solid oak and were hand carved with great detail. The details on the door made no sense at first glance but would play a big part in the shape of things to come.

Mr. Lakur was standing in the doorway wearing an Emerald green, long-sleeved, tapered silk shirt with beige slacks that complemented the tanned leather sandals on his feet. He seemed a bit eager, at least by Ronaw's observation. As Ronaw exited the vehicle, Mr. Lakur reached out to shake his hand and swiftly rushed him into his home with all the enthusiasm of a five-year-old going to Disneyland. Once inside, he proceeded to ask questions.

"Why have you been searching the UKNI-Net system for details about me?"

Ronaw responded calmly, "Your sudden rise to prominence was simply fascinating. I was curious as to how you became a billionaire in such a short time."

Looking about the room Ronaw was rather delighted with the tasteful ornamentation of the room. He pondered though, "What is the purpose of these particular earthen shapes and colors here?"

Mr. Lakur interjected with a somewhat obvious hint of irritation before Ronaw could get entirely off track. So Ronaw explained, "There were an interesting series of events that have led up to today."

Mr. Lakur sat back and listened with great interest to the story. With the discipline of a poker player, he maintained a stoic expression throughout the explanation. However, when Ronaw mentioned Mr. Cantons flying dream sequence, he did seem to shift a little, even though it was barely noticeable. Once Ronaw finished the details Mr. Lakur slowly arose from his Corinthian leather sofa-chair and paced the room quietly in deep thought. Ronaw patiently awaited his response.

While Lakur paced, Ronaw concentrated on the details of the room surroundings. Within the den area, there was an odd but interesting sphere-shaped aquarium that stood in the center of the room.

The sphere was supported by poles that reached down from the ceiling and up from the floor to grasp it along its poles. The supports camouflaged air compressors and filters because they emitted a semi-constant hum. Around the top of the sphere were track lights, four to be exact, on a circular track. Within the sphere was a ring composed of earthen colored clays that rested against the glass leaving a gap, more of a moat around an inner mass. The central mass had to have been specially designed because it just floated and rotated within the moat along the equator of the aquarium.

The aquatic life within the sphere was an odd combination. It was composed of sea horses, angelfish, sea monkeys, and an unusual version of miniature carp. Ronaw noticed a bizarre detail within the aquarium. That detail, within the central land mass, was a miniature tunnel. This tunnel didn't burrow completely through the mass; however, it terminated in what appeared to be a small point of light.

Mr. Lakur asked, "Tell me about the young woman, Karliece. The woman you were with at that restaurant a month ago."

"She was one of my clients with what I thought originally was a vivid imagination. But it turns out that she has a very vivid memory. Which is how I came about locating you."

Lahm smiled at me and said, "Doctor what I'm about to tell you may seem a bit far-fetched, but with all that you've expressed today, I don't think that you'll be too surprised. I have been involved in numerous ventures from bio-genetics to space exploration. My investments include submersible companies just so that they can work from my own designs for a new type of submarine."

"I had no idea that you were into engineering, Mr. Lakur," Ronaw said excitedly.

"Well not by training, but a degree is just a piece of paper saying that you did something by someone else's rules. I've studied engineering as a hobby for some years now. I've also been studying this solar system which, for some odd reason, just doesn't seem right to me."

"I don't think I quite follow you," Ronaw said inquisitively.

"Listen Doc; my family can only be traced through a special government archive, not through public record, at least until after I began to make my mark. The same is true when it comes to several individuals that I've researched thoroughly. All our families seem to have originated within a one-hundred-mile radius of southeastern Tennessee. Next are the dreams that I've had and their correlation with the dreams of other individuals, including those that you spoke of since your arrival. These are dreams that you as a doctor may find to be sort of strange. But, I've been having these dreams ever since I was around twelve years old. They all involve a farm, a little boy around that same age, and a gray dog."

Wait a minute, did he just say the same thing that Karliece said?

Lahm continued, "I've had different dreams of a different sky, filled with flying, crustaceous creatures that were extremely large and malicious. The dreams that I've had most frequently though involve an island; much like the one you see modeled before you within my aquatic-sphere."

Mr. Lakur continued speaking for some time describing events in his life, but Ronaw's mind was still reeling from the mention of the farm, and the twelve-year-old boy with a gray dog. Could there be some connection between Mr. Lakur and himself? This event from his youth that he had merely dismissed as a dream, or flight of fancy, may have in some twisted way have actually happened. Ronaw had to bring himself back to the present as Mr. Lakur continued speaking.

"Doc, look at this structure and tell me whether you think, according to the laws of nature, it could or couldn't exist." Lahm inquired.

"Well, looking at this model, you have before me, I would say that the possibility of such a structures existence is so remote that you have a better chance of conquering the world with a cracker and q-tip," Ronaw said with a snicker.

"Why do you say that professor?" Lahm said in a somber tone.

"Well, from what I understand of gravity and geology, the possibility of such a structure having any kind of stability in the natural order of things is highly improbable. The next is that such a structure would be ripped apart due to the inconsistencies that exist in nature, such as gravity variations, and even wind variations. The perimeter would not be sturdy enough to withstand the impact of any decent-sized object. The constant wave action on the surface of the ocean alone would cause it to fracture and break because there is nothing to stabilize it and keep it away from the inner mass. The ebbing of the tides along with the waves would more than likely cause the perimeter section to crash with the main structure thereby either combining them or obliterating the lesser."

Ronaw got up and walked around the sphere waving his hand along the equator, "Look at it Mr. Lakur, It has no support to hold it in place. The few arms in your model, radiating from its center like the spokes of a wheel provide some form of resistance to gravity or the oceans natural motion, but I don't believe they would be enough, and I presume since they are clear, that they are not supposed to actually be there."

Lakur sat back, and a slight grin crossed his face. He looked at Ronaw and began to laugh.

Observing Ronaws expression of confusion, he said, "Doc, I beg to differ with you on that opinion."

"Why is that Mr. Lakur? What basis do you have, or rather what theory could you have that substantiates your idea?"

"Call me Lahm, Doctor, and to answer your question, I can prove it," Lakur said matter-of-factly.

"With what?" Ronaw shot back.

"One thing at a time Doctor, first things first: the existence of an augmented gravitational field has been documented and proven by scientific organizations as well as scientists within the private sector, some of which I've personally consulted with. The theory is based on the centralization of a gravitational field that is localized and carefully fluctuated and extended throughout key areas in the matrix of the structure to extend that field radially like these spoke-like formations. This field sort of reaches out and pulls evenly at certain points, as well as pushes away intermittently at certain points, providing equilibrium throughout the matrix latticework. Generally, this theory has only held water when dealing with circular structures, and so had been coined CIGRS or Concentric Isotonic Gravitational Repulsion Systems. They can be produced on a scale as small as a dime and in theory, the size of a planetoid, if such a massive contraption could ever truly be constructed."

"An interesting theory; but what kind of proof do you have, Lahm? Your idea verbally seems to be valid but; I would need to see some concrete proof." Ronaw said defiantly.

"Come into my viewing room and I'll show you." Lahm said as he got up from his seat and headed toward a corridor on the opposite side of the room from whence they had entered.

They walked down a long dark corridor that appeared seamless; as if it were carved out of a large solid chunk of black marble that was about fifty feet in length. Ronaw was speechless at the thought of how such a task of this sheer magnitude could have been managed. What drew his attention were some etchings in the walls of the corridor. His mind sifted through his life exposure until it made a connection.

The walls were engraved with what appeared to be maps of galaxies. Two galaxies where highlighted, the Milky Way, which he could easily identify, and another one that sent a shiver down his spine. The second galaxy was labeled M51.

This galaxy resembled the Milky Way, except for a smaller companion galaxy that seemed to be forming along one of its spiraling arms. It was like one galaxy was giving birth to another.

Ronaw remained silent. He just continued down the hallway, making mental notes, into almost complete and utter darkness. He bumped into what he could only guess was Lakur, but when he heard Lakur's voice off to his right, he realized that his assumption was wrong. Ronaw reached out and felt the object, trying to figure out what it was. It was smooth, cool, and supple to the touch. He slid his hand down the side and felt a circular bulge. He could smell leather in the air and assumed that the object had to be some type of leather lounger. The lights came on. The room he had been led into was astounding. It was like a miniature movie theater, with every possible luxury.

"Please have a seat doctor and be amazed by what I'm about to show you," Lakur said with a mischievous grin.
Ronaw sat down in the lounger and glared about his surroundings at all of the gadgets. Once he was comfortably seated, he relaxed a tad-bit and let the smell of leather dance within his nostrils and enter his lungs. The room went black, and he began to hear that annoying whistle that old televisions used to make. The first thing on the screen was a clear undisturbed shot of the ocean, stretching clear off into the horizon. The sounds of seagulls and other seabirds singing their melodious songs caught his attention.

"This, Doctor, is my proof. A little over two months ago, a private ship belonging to Lakur Industries was lost at sea for a few days, about three hundred miles southeast of the Isle of Bermuda. The men on board were the most skilled mariners that I have ever met. There were cameras installed on the aft and stern positions of the boat. These cameras recorded the images that you are seeing." Lakur explained.

The picture grew fuzzy for a minute as if the camera was exposed to some sort of brief but powerful magnetic storm. The sky and surrounding area flooded with clouds, and the cameras shook and rattled as the ships storm warning devices went off. A few moments passed, and the whole scene had reverted back to a serene and clear view.

Ronaw was kind of confused because the voices from the video indicated that they could not get a readout on their position because their guidance link with the orbiting satellite system was going crazy. Based on their own mathematics they could only have traveled about two or three miles along their course. The weird thing was that four to five miles off into the distance was an island that was not there moments before. Everyone on board was pointing at it and trying to figure out where it came from. As they got closer, they estimated that the island was about eight miles in diameter and they were about 6 miles from it. The island had a mountainous region, which appeared to be in excess of two or three hundred feet in elevation.

"The ship was equipped with a solo-chopper. This was a small one manned, high-tech, helicopter, which could be used for aerial observation. This too was equipped with a camera unit and disc recorder. The disc recording was used to eliminate the problem of a magnetic charge, possibly distorting the images that the camera received. One of the shipmates was an ex-pilot, so he was naturally picked to pilot the small craft on its aerial reconnaissance mission of the island. While he was making his trip, the other team of three men were fitted with scuba gear and went diving. They took a camera also. They swam toward the island shore and found, not your normal shelf of down sloping sand, but a flat vertical wall that began about twenty feet below the surface of the water."

"That wasn't the only thing that was interesting Doctor. What was puzzling was how the wall was as smooth as glass but harder than steel. They decided that swimming around the whole island would probably reveal more of the same thing before them, so they dived deeper to see how far down the wall extended." Lahm explained as he and Doctor Ronaw took a sip of water then they returned to watching the video.

The video displayed the divers swimming downward about two hundred feet and found that the wall stopped almost as abruptly as it had started. The bottom of the wall was flat also. It was like an unsupported roof. They had their high beam lights on but for some reason the lights started dimming. After a few moments the lights went out completely and they had to pull out their industrial glow sticks. They proceeded along the ceiling.

Lakur spoke more as the video played on. "Luckily, thanks to my design, the aqua-gear was pressure modulated to regulate their oxygen intake, so they had no problem breathing."

On screen, the team swam through the dark blue, clear ocean for about twenty minutes or so until they reached the interior of the island. The interior was not quite as smooth, nor as inviting. It was dark and dreary, and the light sticks eerie glow made it appear more ominous.

Chapter 12

The first stage of training exercises for the TAS3 uniforms went extremely well. Any and all predicaments were well accounted for. The soldiers adapted to their new living conditions. They learned how to use the automatic laser targeting units that were installed in their helmets for more than just targeting. They were also for focusing and observation as well. There were a few instances of over-extended elbow that developed during hand-to-hand combat exercises, and even a few cases of disorientation in the first few days of training. After the first week, the squad stumbled upon a new and unexpected development.

During the designing stages of the TAS3 units, the scientists included extendible partial shielding for close combat encounters. One shield: for each section of the arms and legs. These could be removed and connected to form one full sized shield for head-on bombardment or, depending on the arrangement, would encase the individual within a protective ball until an assault was over. One of the scientists was there to observe how the soldiers reacted under the stresses of field usage, also, to observe how the soldiers adapted to their suits as one biologically enhanced being.

Early in the development of the TA-series, Dr. Muerte was pulled from a critical scientific assignment involving the concept of bio-interactive-symbiotic metals, or BISM-1development. He was the foremost scientist in that field of Biogenetic research. He theorized that in the early development of new epidermal tissues there is a window of opportunity in which the RNA and DNA sequences can be re-organized to accept, electronically regulated, but independently functioning cell wall integrity shielding. This involved an enormous amount of nano-probes which are injected into the bloodstream and perform surgery on DNA and RNA at the microscopic level.

The outcome of which is a human being with an almost impervious epidermis, which can then be adapted to nearly all environments, including an aquatic one. The only setback was that, for the being to adapt to an aquatic existence, it had to either grow gills or carry around a cumbersome supply of oxygen. The concepts for aquatic soldiers had already been in progress within other regions of the United Nations of Earth's military and scientific establishments.

The only thing that wasn't predicted in all these experiments was the increase in cranial size, the front lobe in particular which was experienced by all of the Squad members. They also reported the ability to vaguely hear or feel the minds of other individuals. Many of the scientists dismissed this concept as a simple side effect of the dosage that the soldiers had taken. The only ones who kept themselves aware were the Squad members themselves.

During the last two weeks of training, the soldiers were given injections, which they were told would slow their metabolisms down so that their bodies could survive on lower amounts of oxygen and at greater depths than what standard divers could withstand. Within moments of the injections, every Squad-member fell unconscious.

Commander Edwards was not being very cooperative when it came to the last of the injections because he felt that he wasn't being told everything. The scientists struggled for more than an hour trying to subdue him before giving up. The head tech finally asked in frustration, "What is it, Commander? Why won't you allow us to give you this last dosage?"

"I want to speak to the head scientist first!" Edwards said sternly. Once they saw that he wasn't going to be cooperative, they promptly requested an audience with the scientist in charge. Dr. Muerte was the man he spoke to. His name seemed familiar in the general's mind, but he couldn't quite think of where he knew the name.

Muerte entered the room and quickly started talking, "Commander, my appointment on this team was not just coincidence. My work in the advanced bio-weaponry corps: for the UNI is incontestable, so what I'm about to tell you is the truth. First of all the TAS3 suits aren't just armor for battle. They are more than just mere pieces of equipment. Those suits alone could subdue and possibly kill in the hands of a six-year-old having a temper tantrum. They are designed for prolonged use and symbiosis. Haven't you noticed that when you're out of the suit for more than ten hours that your body seems to be drawn to the suit?"

Edwards nodded in agreement as Muerte continued, "They are designed to be an extension of each soldier. Once in combat, we don't exactly know what you will be up against, and we can't afford to send our men and women into a battle without every advantage we can think possible. The injection that you've resisted so heavily is not just to slow your metabolism down, it will also transform your body tissue. You will no longer just be a perfect soldier with triple the strength, reflexes, and swiftness; you will also be able to survive aquatically for indefinite periods. In essence, Commander, you and your Squad will be the first real amphibio-sapiens."

Edwards' eyes were wide as Muerte cleared his throat and continued, "I can tell by the expression, of awe, on your face that you don't believe what I'm saying right now but you soon will. Oh! I almost forgot, there are two interesting developments that we noticed during your training. One is that the UKNI-NET computer system will have a direct interface with each of the Squad's members, and the other is an increase in activity in the occipital lobe, which if I'm not mistaken is the lobe in which telepathy is theorized to be located."

Edwards thought to himself, So the voices and feelings we have been picking up are from people around us?

Muerte watched the commanders countenance change before he continued," I see that you're not as slow as many in our government believe most soldiers to be. If you'll have a seat, I have something to show you."

Edwards sat down (still in his TAS3 uniform) and the wall before him seemed to just melt away and was replaced by a large aquarium. At that moment, the thoughts of his mind were clouded with the different thoughts of each of his eighteen-member squad. He focused his mind on blocking out the thoughts of his colleagues and concentrated instead on soothing imagery: waves gently coming and going on the shore, and birds gliding through the air.

The scientist was still talking, but Edwards wasn't listening. His mind was racing in many directions. He began thinking that since he was able to read the thoughts and emotions of the Squad members, as well as project his own thoughts, he should be able to not only read the thoughts of someone, but he may be able to probe deeply within an unprotected mind. Namely, in theory, he should have no problem scanning the doctor for the information that he was not volunteering.

He got up from the chair and glared at Dr. Muerte, who had been going on and on about the advancement and the future of humankind due to the exchange of information, between humans and some undisclosed sources, and then all at once, Muerte became silent. He looked up at Edwards questionably. At first, he felt nothing, but a moment later he felt a gentle tingling sensation that started on the top of his head and spread outward, like a disturbance of the surface of a small pond. The tingling subsided and was replaced by a numbing sensation. The Commander found that the UNI's governing body had been receiving information from a race of beings they call the Nygic that resided in galaxy M104.

The numbness melted away and was replaced by a mild burning. The Nygic had given the government all of the technology that was being used for this mission because they knew that the human military's technology would not be able to handle the current calamity. They decided that they would help but wouldn't directly intervene. They also had the technology to reverse the process that had taken place and was still taking place in those soldiers if they survived the conflict. The burning stopped, and the Commander spoke to Dr. Muerte.

"I will take the injection now and join my Squad in the aquarium."

Dr. Muerte was still flabbergasted by the mind power that he had been subjected to, but since he was already aware of its probability, he could do nothing but accept its existence and make notes.

The Commander was given the injection, and he fought dropping into unconsciousness. His metabolism had spread the substance throughout his system so quickly because his heart was racing from the adrenaline produced during his mind scan of the scientist. As soon as he calmed himself, darkness filled his vision. He thought of childhood and the movies he had watched about UFO encounters with such awe.

He remembered being told that they were all made up by someone's imagination. He remembered his involvement in the now defunct National Security Agency's continual denial of the Roswell, New Mexico, UFO crash, not to mention numerous others. He pondered the thought of what life would be like on other worlds and what those worlds would look like. He thought of the possibilities of the sights never seen by human eyes.

Adair Rowan

Chapter 13

Panning from right to left, the camera gave a breathtaking view of aquatic life. There were all types of fish, seahorses, and coral the size of baseballs. Something was coming at them from a distance. It was glowing and Ronaw could tell from the screen that it was pretty large. He couldn't tell how fast it was moving, but it's size had doubled in less than a minute. Apparently, the object shook up the divers, because the camera shook hastily. The camera zoomed in on another glowing object off in the distance that seemed to be only a reflection of the original object. The diver with the camera turned and swam back towards where they had come from. Every now and then the camera would pan back towards the bright image. An image that was steadily increasing in size. It possessed the dimensions of a humpback whale now. Then, on the last pan, the object pitched left, rolled right, and stopped. During the creature's pause, Ronaw could only see a vague outline of the creature's structure. It was massive and gelatinous. There were eyelike arrays on what he assumed was its head. The creature's body was the wildest thing he'd ever seen. It had a cranial structure similar to that of a giant squid, without tentacles. The torso was broad like that of a stingray, only much larger. There weren't any gills that he could identify. Its whole body was emitting light, some areas brighter than others. The areas he tried to concentrate on were dimmer, allowing him to see more details. Its lower region was an irregular globular mass that pulsated with light. The camera panned around rather abruptly and then went blank.

Lakur turned powered off the video player and turned on the lights.

Ronaw blurted out, "What happened?"

Lakur responded, "From the reports filed by the divers, they swam through a wall made entirely of what they could only describe as sea cucumbers, which they say were suspended from the ceiling down as far as the eye could see into the darkness of the ocean floor. What they found strange was that it wasn't one wall, but three. As they went through the first one, they entered a pool of transparent yellowish goop. It was described as cool enough to give them shivers. This region was only about ten feet wide and they crossed it without incident. The second wall they went through injected them into a reddish liquid. Once inside of this warmer liquid, they swam for a while without coming into contact with anything. Then, out of the blue, one of the more experienced divers started to convulse for no reason. I'm still confused about that; the man has dived far lower depths than this one hundreds of times without any complications. The other divers grabbed hold of him and swam as hard as they could toward the next wall. Before they could reach it though, they too began to convulse. They said they saw the oddest things during their convulsions."

Mr. Lakur paused for a moment with a look of pure excitement on his face. He was short of breath for a moment: his words frozen in his throat. Then he blurted out, "They saw aliens Doc."

"Aliens?" Ronaw repeated back to Lakur suspiciously

"Yes, Aliens," Lakur repeated in kind.

Ronaw began to think that Lakur was perpetrating some kind of hoax, so he responded in his sternest voice, "Mr. Lakur, first of all when a person convulses, they don't remember anything because of a chemical the body produces which wipes out short term memory."

Lakur excitedly retorted, "I know this Doctor, but all of the divers gave separate statements in about tri-eyed semi-transparent, aquatic creatures that came to their rescue. They all state that the beings reached inside of them and pulled out some type of insect-like thing. The insect's rear area was transparent and contained a bluish liquid; the creatures that saved them did so by extracting that liquid and injected it into the convulsing men. Once injected; the convulsions stopped. The tri-eyed beings then escorted the men at hypersonic speed to the next wall. Once there, the creatures swam to and were absorbed into the wall. After that, the wall opened and the divers were sucked out to sea. They said that when they looked behind them, there was no trace of the wall having ever been there."

"Are you sure they weren't drinking before the diving? Because there is no way that something as large as they describe simply disappears."

"That's highly unlikely, Dr. Ronaw. There was no log of liquor being loaded onto the ship at any time. And before you ask, they couldn't 68/+have been using any type of drugs due to the intense screening that I require of all my employees."

"So what of the substance that was injected into the men?"

"Doc, you won't believe this, but it's composed of many protein chains that don't exist on earth. The amino acids are the same as those in the human DNA chain, but their composition is more complicated. We've been trying to find a correlation between it and anything encountered before and we've come up with zilch, nada, nothing even remotely close."

"How are these divers now?"

"The truth is Doc, they are in even better shape than before." Lakur quickly responded.

"What do you mean?" Ronaw queried.

"Well, they seem to have developed a heightened awareness; their memories are almost perfect now in comparison with what they were before this incident. They've read and researched almost everything our computers have to offer and they can crunch numbers close to the rate of our most powerful computers."

"What do you make of all this Mister... I mean, Lahm?"

"The only logical thing I can make of it is that the substance is a biological enhancer of some kind. The one thing I've also noticed is that these divers are now immune to the effects of most drugs. I think that this island should be investigated Doctor, and not by the military." Lahm suggested

"I agree with you, but I think that the others who share your visions should be included in this exploration." Ronaw proposed.

"What If I just send a squad out to the island to see if it's safe and then we bring the others?" Lahm advocated.

"Please, uh, Lahm, this discovery could be something that all of you are meant to be a part of, so please, allow me to assemble the others."

Mr. Lakur sat in deep thought for a moment and then nodded in agreement.

Ronaw departed from the Lakur retreat in the cruiser that he had arrived in with much on his mind and much more to do. Lakur had provided him with a video to show the others with similar visions. Dr. Ronaw sincerely hoped that the recording would convince them to join his and Lakur's expedition to the island.

At first, Ronaw took time to appreciate and

truly enjoy the ride of such a stunning vehicle. The Land cruiser rode so well that he didn't turn on the radio. He just focused on the steady hum of its quiet engine and felt for the gentle bumps of the road beneath the extra wide tires. And changing lanes was so smooth; Ronaw felt like he was on a yacht, gently swaying on a small wave.

Until the island again invaded upon his solitude. Now lost in thought, Ronaw pondered the situation. It was becoming more intriguing every day. He began to wonder about the divers. If they weren't hallucinating, and if what they said was true, then all of mankind would be in for one heck of a shock. All those religious fanatics would be shocked to death by proof of life elsewhere, not mentioned (in specific detail), in their bibles.

And why were all these people connected? What was it that was found in the blood sample from the injured child? Why am I also having these strange reoccurring dreams? His last thought, a thought that made him considerably anxious, echoed the loudest: Am I somehow connected to these people, to the island... to life forms that, prior to today, I hadn't a clue even existed?

Chapter 14

The government took some inmates from death row, housed in a hardcore, top security lifer institution and transported them to a black budget facility located in the northeastern region of Tennessee. They were given a choice, die within the next week or take their chances on a long shot opportunity. All but a handful agreed to go to the then-undisclosed location.

The facility was on the Boone Lake Peninsula. It was highly guarded with over three hundred individual soldiers and a laser tracking system. This facility, covering over two miles in diameter, enclosed an intricate maze and survival course buried several hundred feet underground. Each prisoner was given the choice of weapons from swords and daggers to semi and fully automatic weaponry with as many clips as they could carry. They were also injected with miniature Personnel Tracking Beacon's so that the monitoring team could keep track of their progress. They were told one thing by the contact giving instructions, "SURVIVE THE MAZE."

When some asked what their reward was, the answer was a full pardon, new identities, relocation, and financial security for the rest of their natural lives. There were thirty men in all.

Those who were experienced hunters and military trained marksmen led the pack and those with close quarter expertise followed. The thinkers were kept within the middle of the crowd. They never even asked what they were up against.

The convicts were delivered to the top of the facility by helicopter. The entrance and the only way they could go in was via an elevator door. The individuals with firearms were first on the elevators and into the maze. A group of fully equipped inmates (tagged group A by the observers), approximately fifteen, headed toward the entrance of the maze. They walked along the linoleum passageway listening to their own footsteps echo back at them from a distance. The next group was coming down the elevator. They all carried walkie-talkies. Once everyone was inside the maze, the scientist conducting the exercise deactivated the elevator. The elevator stopped humming with electricity and came to rest at the bottom of the shaft with a dull thump. After they exited the elevator, the power in the elevator was cut. Observing this, the prisoners organized themselves into their respective groups of fifteen, which then broke into groups of five. The first group came to the fork of the maze and headed towards the left, the second cluster went to the right. The left corridor was brightly lit for about a hundred feet or more. The right corridor however only had lights every fifty or so feet. The dark areas were intimidating.

The group in the left corridor proceeded through their tunnel at a brisk speed while those in the other tunnel moved on with extreme caution. In the distance, both groups heard hissing sounds. Sort of like air escaping from a tire or two King Cobras fighting. The sound amplified until it seemed to be coming from every direction. Both groups formed a circle with the armed men on the outside. In the lighted tunnel, the lights began to flicker on and off. The flickering started once every five seconds, but the interval between flickers dwindled until it felt like a strobe light in a nightclub.

The group in the darkened tunnel heard gunfire. They stopped cold. The screaming was horrible. It was the sound of men fighting for their lives. This time death had an actual shape, and apparently a bad temper. The armed men moving through the lit tunnel saw creatures moving so fast that they were just misshapen blurs moving in their distance. They never got a clear view due to the flickering lights, but everyone in the group had seen enough to be fearful. One man raised his gun and took aim at the mid-section of one of the shapes coming toward him. As he looked through his scope, he could see in greater detail what the creature looked like.

He thought, "Damn, they almost look human."

He re-aimed his weapon at the abnormal head of the creature and pulled the trigger. There was no sound but the echo of the gunshot throughout the chamber. The creature went down. It did not fall, exactly, it sort of just sat down in a kneeling position with its abnormally long fingers cradling its head. He turned his back and took aim at another creature. Behind him, the creature raised its head, stood up and focused in on the man with the gun. The inmate saw motion out the corner of his eye and turned to look at the thing that was now standing right before him. The clothing on the beast looked like some type of futuristic armor. It had an insignia at the upper region of the arm. A double parted circle with a multi-parted globe on the inside; the ends of each half of the parted circle had some type of multi-segmented cones inserted. It was not moving, it was just standing there, so the inmate went back to randomly firing at the creatures flashing around them. The creature took to the air from its standing position and inverted itself to an upside-down standing position on the ceiling, about twenty feet from the group. It's mind searching for the mind of the man with the weapon. Then the man with the gun stopped firing at the other creatures coming through the tunnel. He felt his blood, as it seemed to boil within his veins. His heart raced as he panned his firearm around to the direction from which the first creature had come, but it wasn't there. He looked around and around but didn't see the creature. The creature was hanging from the ceiling by its feet, like a bat. No one had seen it jump with blinding speed to its resting place overhead. They did not know that it was there, above them, watching, deciding whom to attack.

The other creatures attack on the group abruptly stopped and they seemed to vanish into thin air. None of the group had actually been harmed, just scared half to death. The creature on the ceiling reached behind its back with elongated fingers as the material liquefied at its lower back and bulged to issue forth a flat Frisbee sized object. Once the object was removed, the liquid re-solidified and covered its back. The creature extended its large arms. The fingers elongated more to fine sharp points. The massive legs of the creature bulged as it pulled its upper body toward the ceiling like a cat getting ready to pounce on a mouse. The next thing that happened took but a few moments.

Adair Rowan

Chapter 15

Dr. Ronaw was walking through the airport toward the terminal where the plane was being refueled for his flight back home when he had that feeling again, like someone was watching him. He turned around and saw nothing unusual.

A group of little old ladies fussed at each other about who was supposed to bring the Clue game for the flight. Passengers were conversing across the isles. The terminal personnel rushed to and fro frantically.

And then he noticed a group of men with black suitcases. Not only did they have black suitcases, but they also wore super dark sunglasses. He found that somewhat odd, because it was late in the evening and the windows had a high level of tint. As personnel led him to his plane, he noticed that the gentlemen were still behind him. They were trying to blend in, but their efforts at concealing themselves were so poor that he almost laughed.

Ronaw was already anxious about the mystery that had dropped into his lap; however, he knew that he should stop and find out what they wanted.

He stopped in his tracks and when the men were closer to him, he turned around and asked, "Excuse me, is there a problem gentlemen?"

Rather nonchalantly, the tallest of the group responded, "There could be if you make a scene Doctor."

"What reason would I have to make a scene sir?" Ronaw shot back.

The man shifted his weight from one leg to the other before saying calmly, "Doctor Ronaw, we need a moment of your time."

In response, Ronaw proposed, "feel free to join me on my plane, it is secure if there is a need."

The man he was talking with tapped his watch twice, and three other black suits converged on their position. They encircled Ronaw and proceeded with him onto his plane. Once everyone boarded and the door was sealed the largest gentleman spoke. He had a southern accent like he was from Tennessee or Georgia maybe.

"Doctor, we have reason to believe that what you are investigating could affect the security of our Nation."

***

"This is Sheriff Jordan to all cars, Jordan to all cars please report in," Jordan bellowed over the radio in sequence after switching to emergency frequency four. Sheriff Jordan was shaken by what had taken place.

Perspiration clung to his forehead like warm icing on a cake, struggling to hold its position against the pull of gravity. The eight squad cars for his county were all responding.

The sheriff then stated his instructions, "All roads and houses in the forested area, for a five-mile radius should be evacuated immediately."

One of the deputies asked, "Why do we need to do that Sheriff?"

Jordan almost tore his head off, "Bratton, just do as I say! This is an emergency."

Catching his breath, Jordan continued a little more calmly, "I'll brief you all in detail a bit later, but I stress that you make sure you block off the roads so that no one wanders into the woods on accident."

The radio was silent for about five minutes until they heard a distress call from another deputy who was close to one of the creek beds.

"This is Lomax, uh... I need a bit of a hand here. I seem to have run across; well, the largest damn uh bug? I've ever seen, and it's got a few friends. I'm near the creek beds about a quarter mile south on Asbury road."

"Dammit!!! The sheriff shouted as he swung the car around on the little dirt road and started back down the road they had been traveling on. He keyed his mic and urgently requested, "All deputies, converge on the last known position indicated by deputy Lomax. You will, I repeat, you will need to unlock your secondary trunk weapon to assist."

His pulse was racing with the excitement, the thrill of having to actually do something and some panic based on what he recently experienced. Antoine sat there with determination etched on his face.

He bounced with the motions of the car as they rocketed down the dirt roads at about seventy miles per hour. At that speed, they felt almost every crevice and dip the road had to offer. The Sheriff's antique Eighty-three Chevy Impala rattled and grunted, like a child wrestling, as it ate up the miles toward their destination.

The Sheriff's face was tense with wrinkles in his forehead that looked like they were carved from mahogany stone. The veins around his temples were. They rounded the dirt driveway and almost sideswiped another police vehicle.

The sheriff yanked the wheel to the right, and at the same time adjusted the gas and brakes until he drifted his car around the vacated vehicle, all the while cursing, "Who in the hell left their car there?"

It was at that moment that he remembered ordering the other deputies to block off the roads. Suddenly, gunshots rang out. Antione and the sheriff both ducked for cover as they came to a stop. The sheriff scrambled out of the car and hid behind it. Antione ran around the front of the card and what he saw made his stomach draw up into a tight ball, and reflexively he slumped over with a dry hurl as he turned toward the Sheriff and motioned him over. The sheriff shuffled towards Antione and looked past him only to see the brutally mangled and mutilated body of Lomax resting on a tree stump in the middle of a clearing. The other officers were shooting toward the upper branches of the trees. Jordan and Antione flew back around the car and dashed into the clearing.

Jordan called out repeatedly, "Hold your fire damn it!!"

The deputies fired a few shots more toward the treetops before they shouldered their weapons.

"What the hell happened here?" Jordan forcefully inquired.

"Sheriff, you won't believe it!" the officer stated. He was broad shouldered with a hard-chiseled looking chin. The sweat raced down the sides of his face in the muggy heat.

"There were these things, they were like huge bugs, like in those classic Godzilla movies of the seventies. They were just sitting there taking bites out of Lomax like he was a steak. It appears that after a few bites he must've died, cause by the time I arrived he wasn't moving as they munched on him, Sheriff."

The other deputy finished up the report. One of them had wet his pants in all the excitement. This deputy was a small, wiry fella with a short-faded haircut. He'd lost his hat somewhere too.

The sheriff, on the other hand, was thinking

rather furiously.

"What the hell is going on Sheriff?" Both deputies grunted in unison. They were breathing hard and gripping their AP 50's like an addict clenching a crack pipe. Antione looked at the sheriff, one eyebrow raised. The sheriff nodded his approval.

Chapter 16

The figure released its foothold on the ceiling of the corridor and flipped upright as it landed amid the first group of inmates. The creature swung the Frisbee-like object and released it into the air. It flew from the creature's hand with a purring sound. The object crackled with static electricity it seemed to collect as it sliced through the air and beveled into the wall.

The inmates were standing there in amazement as the wall began to cave in. The automatic weapons they were holding became hard to hold on to. Something was pulling at the weapons. They struggled to maintain their only means of defense. Three of the guns wrested themselves free and sailed through the air toward the beveled area of the wall. The other two weapons were being held firmly by rather large men. They were trying to get leverage by leaning against the pull of the magnetized region of the corridor.

The men were grunting and yelling, "Get that damn thing, cut it down man!"
The creature was just standing there with its arms extended. Two of the men were pulled towards the wall, but they were no longer playing tug of war with their guns. The guns were now pulling them

and soon they hung in the air like kites. They pulled their knives and cut the shoulder straps so that they could be free to formulate some type of an attack or defense against the creature, which had appeared from out of nowhere. It didn't move.

The inmates de-sheathed impressive blades. One held a Bowie knife, the other an Indian hunting knife with an intricately detailed leather wrapped handle. These knives were apparently made of ceramic as the magnet had no effect on them. One of the creatures dashed through the crowd of men. As it did so, everybody swung toward the creature. The cling of multiple impacts of metal on metal sang through the corridor. The creature didn't even attempt to block any of the blows; and when it came to a dead stop, there wasn't a scratch to be seen anywhere.

The Creature just stood there; there was no face. There was an insect-like helmet, with indentations indicating a ghastly facial structure. The helmet just sort of melted into a neck with a seamless connection along the collar. The inmates surrounded the thing, it still didn't move. The men walked in a circle around the beast, tossing their weapons from hand to hand. Their actions were only to show that they weren't afraid of what they'd just seen. The creature began to follow their motion by turning with their movements. Its gaze regularly came to rest on the largest of the inmates. He was muscle upon muscle upon a frame of steel. Noticing the creature's apparent lack of interest, one of the men dived in toward the creature's back. Before the inmate could even tell what was going on, the creature grabbed its attacker by the arm that held the weapon and snapped it in four places. The inmate yelled out in excruciating pain. He dropped to his knees and curled himself up into a fetal position cradling his contorted arm.

The creature just looked at him and returned its gaze to the other four challengers. They turned and began to run. The creature dived towards the nearest two inmates and swung its arms in a slicing motion toward their legs. Both men lost a leg from the kneecap down and fell to the ground, screaming like pigs at the slaughterhouse.

The other two men continued down the corridor at their top speeds. They were hoping that the exit was somewhere close. Little did they realize the distance they covered wasn't quite a mile. Frantically checking behind, themselves as they ran, they completely missed the two figures standing in the pathway before them. They probably wouldn't have seen them anyway.

The two figures were like chameleons and seemed to be an extension of the wall. One was short and thick with a feminine build. The other was tall but slender in comparison to the creature at the other end of the passageway. It was male, you could tell by the structure of its broad shoulders and lack of protrusions on the upper torso.

Both creatures swiftly and stealthily leapt into the air and pierced the wall with their claws. Leaning their bodies in an angle they stretched the claws of their free arms out toward the running inmates. There they hung with the ease of spiders, their claws embedded easily in the wall like it was a lump of cheese.

Their extended claws were razor sharp and aimed to strike just below the Adam's apple of the approaching inmates. Just before contact, the inmates turned to catch a glimpse of death in its personified form. They started to scream but before the sound could escape, talons sliced completely and cleanly through their throats destroying the larynx.

There was a small sound from the blades impact with the brief amount of bone present in the human's necks. Their heads fell back like ripe melons, bouncing a few times and coming to rest with an expression horror forever frozen upon their faces. The bodies continued down the hallway, spouting blood along the way with the hiss of air escaping lungs and venting through soggy passageways. The bodies ran about ten feet before collapsing on top of each other in a shivering heap of flesh and bodily fluids.

The two beings released their grip on the wall and glided to the floor with almost no sound. The heads of the two men were resting in small pools of blood. Eyes sightlessly rolled around in eye sockets, unable to focus as the brain quickly ran out of oxygen. The creature that sliced off the inmate's legs squatted between the two men as they lay along the wall in shock. Its attention was turned toward the man lying in a fetal position in the center of the floor. The other two of its kin were quietly proceeding closer. Upon their arrival, they stood almost at attention as the creature rose slowly between them.

In the darkened tunnel; the remaining small group of inmates were so still; the sound of breathing could barely be heard. They stood in a tight huddled bunch, every eye working furiously to see anything off in the distance. The walls began to shudder, but the floor didn't. They stood there in confusion as what appeared to be some type of hand, or claw, or something, slowly extended outward from within the wall. It was long like the talons of an eagle. A massive forearm, then a shoulder and massive torso followed the space behind the clawed hand. The creature that came out of the wall was alien, but also, human-like in appearance. The neck had an emblem engraved on it in what appeared to be gold plating. It was circular with cones of some kind. The creature's body shimmered. It stopped and turned back toward the wall and disappeared in much the same way as it had come into the passageway. The inmates were so busy staring at the one in front of them that they hadn't noticed the other three behind them that began to reverse their motion also. Then just as amazingly as they had appeared, they disappeared, slowly dissolving into the walls.

Chapter 17

"National Security?" Ronaw responded suspiciously.

"Yes Doctor, national security. Your activities for the last month have been closely monitored." The agent calmly answered.

"I don't believe I understand."

"You see Doctor, the information that you've been trying to obtain has been kept under wraps for several political as well as social reasons, of which I am not at liberty to disclose at this time. What we have been instructed to do is to assist you in your work under the strict condition that what you see, hear, and experience must never be made public knowledge."

"Wait a minute, I haven't seen anything or experienced anything, so I'm still at a loss in regarding whatever it is that you're talking about." Ronaw shot back.

"Doctor, please stop playing games. We're here to acquire your services for a limited time. You will be compensated very well if all goes according to plan."

Frustrated, Ronaw replied, "If all what goes as planned?

Ignoring the question, the agent continued, "To be blunt Dr. Ronaw, you've stumbled upon something that most of our people have missed."

"Again, what are you talking about?" Ronaw asked again.

"Our team has the ability to access any files that Psy. Docs create or access with UKNI-NET... records that we investigate regularly and thoroughly. Within the last month, you've been involved in a case that our department has been trying to solve for the last twenty years.

Ronaw was bewildered and curious at the same time, but he remained quiet, allowing the agent to divulge what he thought Ronaw had "uncovered."

The agent forged ahead, "Doctor, a little over twenty years ago our surveillance network of satellites and observatories around the world recorded two objects piercing the Earth's atmosphere. One object left the earth, the other one did not. If my memory serves correctly, the object that did not leave the Earth's atmosphere was reported heading slightly beyond the Bermuda triangle. There was no record of any explosion by satellite, nor any impact points along the object's projected path."

"So, what does this have to do with me? I'm a therapist, not an astronomer."

"Doctor, be quiet please!" The agent was obviously nervous by the way he kept pacing back and forth within the confines of the plane. He kept rending his hands as if he was trying to get something off them.

"Doctor, the government at that time had no way of knowing what the objects were. The military bases in that particular region were understaffed and under-equipped due to the cutbacks in arms of that time period. Also, those bases were not working under one government, which really doesn't make a difference right now. The other object, however, was recorded leaving our solar system at an exceptionally high speed. We've had scientists, the most brilliant and the most eccentric, to calculate and hypothesize the direction from which it came and its destination. The best theory to date is the idea that the object was indeed an alien craft which came from a galaxy about five light years away."

Interrupting once more Ronaw forcefully said, "So I'm asking again, what does this have to do with me?"

"Well, Doc. at almost the same time that you started searching into the files about certain entries, another object entered our region in space. Its measurements were twice that of the object that escaped the earth's magnetic pull over twenty years ago, and its destination seemed to be at that time, the earth. Along its path, it released half of its mass into the gas giant of Jupiter.

Ronaw eyes widened, he couldn't breathe.

No way am I in the middle of a lost episode of the X-files. Am I going to be the hero or the smoker dude that always covered things up? He thought.

Ronaw sat back and for clarification asked, "So you are actually saying what?"

"Come on Doctor, you're bright, and you know exactly what I'm saying." The agent pressed.

"I believe I do, but I still don't see where I fit into all this." Ronaw shot back.

"Doctor, we believe that some of your most recent clients, as well as the other patients you've been investigating are somehow linked to this occurrence and the incident which happened over twenty years ago." The agent said matter-of-factly.

The agent paused for a second and then excitedly added, "Oh! And by the way, we've come across a rumor that provides new evidence of some island that we have yet to locate."

"So, let me get this much straight. You think that alien life forms visited earth about twenty years ago." Ronaw started

"Correct." The agent confirmed.

"You also believe that this same life-form or object has returned for some unknown reason." Ronaw declared.

"Right," the agent affirmed.

"You think that my patients, some island, and this unknown craft are somehow connected."

"By golly Doctor, I think you've got it." The other men in dark suits glanced at one another and slightly smiled.

The agent finally made his point, "We need you to assist in the gathering of the people that we have identified, as well as those that you've located. Since you already have a connection with the gentleman you met with earlier today; Mr. Lakur, we want to assist you all in creating this expedition."

Ronaw thought to himself, *this is the opportunity to find out if all my years of reading books and watching TV shows about alien life would be of some value.*

He sat back and ruminated for a while, trying to make them sweat, but at the same time, they knew that he wouldn't pass this up.

Adair Rowan

Chapter 18

The room was silent. The air was tinted with a tad of potpourri. The sun was fading away into the underworld as night overcame the city. One candle provided a soft glow that reached out from the center of the room, losing its strength the further it went from the candle falling a few feet short of the walls.

There they sat, in a circle, holding hands. The windows were closed, and all of the electronic appliances were unplugged to prevent interference. These six individuals of different ethnicities, ages, and sexes listened to the sounds of each other's breathing. This wasn't a ritual; it was a necessity. They began this about six months before.

All of them were drawn together by a shared and unique experience. An experience that no one had been able to understand, nor find any reason for the connection besides the experience alone. Through this meditation, they also found that they could project the thoughts and feelings regarding the experience into each other's minds. It was easy, almost too easy and no one could explain why this was possible.

It was an amazing coincidence how six random individuals, happened to move into the same city, all around the same time. It was surprising that they all knew of The Island; however, no one knew how to find it. They all knew of the tunnel, but not what it meant. They also knew of the sinister, malignant feeling that came from the dark, eyes of an ominous creature in the shadows. They all knew of the farm, but no one knew what it added up to, so they all came together once a week to speculate and try to provide more details that might enlighten each of them. They also hoped that the meetings might possibly bring them closer to an explanation of what was happening.

John was a Head Paramedic with an exemplary record. Lu Tan was a law student at Florida A&M with honor courses in biology and chemistry. Shonda was a pharmacist and made a very good living as a regional pharmacist manager for a local twenty-seven-store chain. Charles was recently appointed CEO of the largest Security enforcement agency within the mid-Floridian region. Lameka was a Data Entry Supervisor and Computer programmer with the leading software company. Lana was pre-med at Florida A & M also, focusing her major on genetics.

During the gatherings, they all took note that they had the same physician, lived within a sixty-mile radius of one another while living in Tennessee and that they all moved to Florida within a three-month period. They also could not get the image of this little boy, with a dog, on a farm out of their minds. So, this weekend, as previously planned, they all agreed to caravan back to their hometown and see if they could locate this farm and find out more about it.

***

His breathing was shallow. It got deeper and deeper until his eyes finally opened. Julius Sr. got up from the bed gently as to not awaken the graceful figure lying beside him. She was so beautiful with sandy brown hair, graying in teasing streaks at the temples. Her skin was still as flawless as the day they met. Her high cheekbones and full lips, big beautiful brown eyes, and a slender, graceful neck complemented her package.

He watched as her chest rose and fell with each breath. He wanted her. The thought of her warm body against his was still exciting. Her soft skin, the taste of her tongue in his mouth. He slipped back into bed and kissed her gently on the forehead and ran his fingers through her hair. She mumbled something under her breath and smiled slyly. Her eyes fluttered open quickly. Apparently, she was awake, playing possum.

"Oh, so you are awake!" Julius said with a smile as his hand escaped from her hair, flitted down along the nape of her neck and over the top of her shoulder.

Maudine moaned her response, loving how her husband desired her at seemingly all hours.

Her hands slid up her body to rest on his head, and she pulled him closer to her tenderly.

Thirty years of marriage and they still had the passion of young lovers, stealing time. They joined together, their bodies performing a symphony of songs in harmony. Beat after beat and bar after bar, they were as one until they reached the climactic resolution of the song. They both lay back, snuggling up in each other's arms and smiling at one another.

"Good morning, Mrs. Canton."

"Good morning to you, Mr. Canton."

Mr. Canton's cell phone began to vibrate behind him, on the nightstand next to the bed. He rolled away from his wife slightly and grabbed it, casually answering, "Hello!"

As Julius listened to the phone call, he sat up from his initial position and put his feet on the floor. "Uh hunh," he said. Maudine lay across the bed with her back to him with her eyes partially closed.

"And you say we're all invited?" Julius asked the unknown caller.

"Ok, I guess you can count us in, I mean I will check with our children, but I know that we would love to take a cruise on a private yacht at Mr. Lakur's expense," Julius said. His wife rolled over to only see his back to her. She sat up and slid next to him just as he was disconnecting the call and asked, "What was that about a cruise?"

***

There they sat within a twelve by twenty-foot room filled with monitors and computer data links. The four observers watched in awe at the quickness and viciousness of their latest creations. This was something they invested considerable time and resources into for the past eighteen years. These four individuals had requested the privilege of seeing their creations in action.

They marveled at the displays. They also resented the use of human sacrifices, which is what the inmates were. Over thirty men had been shipped to this facility like pigs to slaughter. Yes, they were given weapons, but they had no understanding of what it was they were about to face.

The squad made mincemeat of the first group of inmates that had entered into the training passageways. Two men decapitated and three suffered from removed limbs. Then the attackers made a silent, confusing retreat. Why had they just vanished? The last group of inmates was almost at the exit and their chance at a new life. What had caused the squad to disappear?

They sat there watching the displays in utter confusion, so no one was paying attention to the wall behind them. It quivered like a flag in the wind, and then it rippled like the surface of a pond. Sharp claw-like protrusions emerged from within the wall. The sharp things converged and merged into two groups of five forming the fingers of hands, which then gave way to massive arms.

Behind the massive arms came the enormous legs and odd-looking three-toed feet. In between the three toes, was some type of material that appeared to stretch from the tips of the toes like the webbing of a duck's feet.

The creatures were a mixture of male and female beings. They all stepped away from the walls in perfect synchronization. In the middle of the line stood one creature that looked identical to all the others in every way except for the color of its skin. It was the only one that had a copper tinged with gold appearance out of the group.

It also had some kind of markings on its chest. A large dissected orb within a bi-symmetrically cut circle that ended with a cone on each end of the half circles.

Chapter 19

Just as LuTan was entering his small studio apartment, he heard the telephone ringing. Thinking it might be someone important, he tossed his books toward the couch and high-stepped his way to the counter-bar wall mount where the phone was.

Shonda was having a late lunch when she received an emergency page from her answering service. She was extremely curious. Since she was at lunch, she casually made her way to her office and asked her secretary to hold all calls. She called the service and was surprised to find out that she had been left a plane ticket and given instructions to be ready to leave this weekend. At first, she was shocked, then a tad-bit angry, considering that she didn't have any idea who was making the request. She soon, however, settled down when she heard the vague message left with the instructions. The message stated,

"Secluded island investigation: research involving the similarities between participants, including, but not limited to visions of an underwater tunnel."

Shonda almost dropped the phone. Exasperated, she stood stock still, her head spinning in so many directions. Finally gathering her bearings, Shonda made plans to go on this special journey. Her boss did not have any qualms with her finally taking a vacation.

Charles Kelly was bored when he received his phone call. Being head of security was cool, but it wasn't all that he thought it would be. He had a big cushy office with a nice view, a healthy ficus tree, but no excitement. He missed being on the beat. He loved the nervous anticipation of not knowing what would happen next. He missed walking around with his wits pushed to the limit. On the edge of it all is where he wanted to be. His secretary put the call through.

Charles answered, "Mr. Kelly here, how can I help you?

The person on the line stated, "You will be receiving a very important fax in a few moments. Please read through the details within said fax and plan accordingly. If there are any questions, please call the number within the fax. Your travel details will be listed as well. Also, please do not hesitate to take this short hiatus from work. This will be very beneficial to you and your group."

Charles stood over his fax machine and read the papers as they printed out. After doing so, he pressed the intercom and told his secretary to make a note to all employees that he would be gone for about a week and that they were to report to his assistant. Then he looked through his phone for Lameka and Lana's numbers. Once found, he called them on a conference line to see if they had all received a mysterious call.

Lameka and Lana sat on the phone line silent for a few moments before Lameka asked, "Eerie, isn't it?"

Charles cleared his throat and answered, "More like strange, but I'm going. I've got to know."

Lana still hadn't said anything. She was busy struggling in her mind with whether or not she should tell them about her last episode. She quietly responded, "Guys . . . I have a funny feeling that something significant will happen, but I also have an ominous feeling."

Charles sighed loudly.

Lameka was silent for a moment before she answered, "Lana, I plan on going, and my advice is that you come along also. We're all in this together right?"

In unison Charles and Lana both responded, "Right" and then the line was rather quiet.

Charles broke the silence and stated, "Sometimes in life, there are things that are beyond our normal understanding, but we must take the journey to its conclusion."

***

The doctors were shaken by the silence in which the squad had surrounded them.

One of the scientists exclaimed, "Holy cow! Where did they come from?"

Another scientist apprehensively said, "After what I just saw them do to those inmates, I can only wonder what they will do to us!"

The golden-skinned squad member stepped forward. The material along the neck of the creature began to vibrate, creating a hum in the room. The creature placed its hands on its head and proceeded to pull its head off. The doctors were all shocked by what they witnessed. The neck covering material made a gurgling sound and fell back into place after relinquishing its hold on the helmet. The creature underneath was humanoid, but not wholly human. Its eyes were incandescent. Its cranium had an abnormal size and shape to it.

Commander Edwards projected his human appearance into their minds, and the doctors all stood there with their mouths open.

They were silent as the commander's words echoed directly into their minds. "Where are the targets that we need to confront?"

The entire group of scientists robotically pointed toward the computers. The screen depicted an activity tracer that curved southeasterly across Tennessee. The trail had expanded in small areas only to re-converge into one fine trail.

Edwards slipped the helmet back on and his suit recompressed for battle. The heads-up terminal was giving coordinates for the last known area of contamination. Edwards turned to the squad, who, at his nod, submerged into the surrounding walls.

Concentric Relations: Unknown Ties

Adair Rowan

Chapter 20

The Aquaticus was beautiful. She was graceful, sleek and luxurious. If she were a woman, she would've been queen Nefertiti. She was four hundred feet long: a semi-triangular floating oasis. The Lakur emblem branded the vessel on either side. While gawking at the massive, sheer beauty of the ship, the fifty or so passengers were hustled aboard. There was a shaky silence that overtook them as they joined the twenty-man crew.

The captain was a stout fellow that stood at firm six-foot-three inches and possessed a rugged beard. Today he wore a black beret, creased khakis and a stiffly starched white polo shirt. His appearance was breathtakingly attractive to the women as many eyed him voraciously.

The crewmembers were all well trained and seasoned seamen. The youngest of the crew was a twenty-five-year-old ex-Navy seal. He had just gotten tired of fighting the terrorist war and not having the opportunity to live a normal life. He was in top physical condition, and his skills as a SEAL came in handy from time to time.

The Aquaticus' crew personally escorted each of the passengers to their appointed cabins as *The Aquaticus* hoisted anchor and set off from the

Lakur port, located on Merritt Island in Florida. It traveled south until it reached the St. Lucie Inlet and then altered its course toward the Bermuda isles.

The captain knew they were headed toward the outer tips of an underwater mountain range called the Nares Plain, which began approximately four hundred miles off the coast of Bermuda. It was located within the well-known region called the Bermuda triangle. He was curious as to why they were taking such a strange route to get there. Being in the employ of Mr. Lakur had been very advantageous, so he asked very few questions. He was also wondering about all of the "experimental" diving gear that required over half of the ship's payload area.

After settling into their cabins, Mr. and Mrs. Canton took time to soak in their surroundings. They lay stretched across their queen-sized bed staring at the paintings on the walls and the ceiling. The cabin had an outdoorsy feel to it. They noticed that when the curtains were shut and the lights were off; little dots on the ceiling formed a pattern resembling stars or constellations. The star scene was vaguely familiar, but neither of them could determine why. They also took the time to play with the Micro Laser computer that was located just off to the right side of the bed. The computer offered a menu of things to choose from. They selected music first and ran down the list to the jazz collection. They both loved Jazz. They'd met in a little jazz club located in the southern suburbs of their hometown. On that particular night, a live band by the name of Sultry was playing their rendition of Ben Webster's tender tune Stormy Weather. It was why they'd adopted Stormy Weather, as their couple song.

The Cantons reminisced about the good ole' days as they danced to it now. They swooped and bobbed around the cabin like they did when they were still wet behind the ears.

Charles was reading the menu on his computer and chose first to see the list of the passengers. Some of the names seemed slightly familiar, but he didn't know why. After that, he checked out the route of their cruise. Feeling as if he had an inkling about where they were going, Charles dismissed it. The mysterious place he had dreamt about did not appear on any maps. He laughed at himself. Realizing how silly this all appeared, he decided to call Lana and Lameka to see if they'd learned anything.

Lana was stepping out of her shower when the video-cam's neon blue bulb demanded her attention. She hit the FL button on the monitor, which allowed her to see who was calling before she answered the call). Once she saw that it was Charles, she pushed the RT indicator on the terminal.

Cheerfully she answered, "Hey Charles, what's up?"

There was a moment of silence between

them as he took in the fact that she was standing before her camera with next to nothing on. Lana blushed a little at his distracted gaze and eyes that were so wide, they almost popped out of his head.

"Uh, I'm sorry uh, Lana, call me back when you're dressed," Charles stammered.

"Charles, you know that you need to quit. You are so silly." Lana gleefully replied.

"Well, I was just wondering if you had any news or any clue as to where we're headed?" Charles inquired

"Not yet but as soon as I do, you'll be the first to know; talk to you in a while hunh?" Lana replied

"Yeah, humph, see ya," Charles said, as he terminated the call.

***

"The natives are getting a bit restless!" Lakur explained to Dr. Ronaw.

"Well, Lahm, it's your show, so I think you should proceed with explaining to the guests what is going on." Dr. Ronaw responded.

Lakur pushed the all quarters button on his desk. This little button connected his Vid-link feed with all of the computers in the cabins and the PA System on *The Aquaticus* at one time.

Lakur punched a few keys on the keyboard and said, "My dear guests and new friends, we all share something in common; a vision if you will.

148

A vision; which forewarned us of something that is coming. Something that we may not have told too many people about. Well . . . I've found out that one of the many things I've dreamt about, many if not all of you have as well."

Lakur could feel the collective gasps on the ship as he continued, "The place that I have envisioned is a reality. I'm about to show you a videotape of what we have all only seen in our dreams. Where we are going on this excursion is into the unknown." He fell silent.

On screen, the viewers saw him type a command into his terminal and allowed them to see the footage that he had shown Dr. Ronaw. Once the video was complete Lakur appeared on the Vid Link again once more to sign off.

Calmly, Lakur stated, "I know that this is a lot to absorb, so you have the rest of the evening to do so. Please write down your questions overnight and present them in the morning."

No one left his or her quarters that night. The captain, having dived in many of the most interesting places the world has to offer, was even caught off-guard by what he saw. Many prepared a list of things to ask others. They all felt excited and apprehensive at the same time. They wanted to know it all, but they were also fearful about what they may find.

Adair Rowan

Chapter 21

The SQUAD was transported from the base in upper Tennessee to Fort Gillen, Ga. and onwards to JFK space center. They never left their special biome-quarters. They were then scheduled for a briefing before they left for marine marker 5795. The SQUAD was quiet but anxious. They had trained all their lives for this, their moment in the spotlight. Their bodies had been scientifically mutated, molded, like clay. They were the best and only team for such a mission. If they failed, mankind could and possibly would be annihilated. They had the New World Order's stamp of approval and good faith, and boy would they need it.

* * *

As Antione explained to the deputies what had happened, the Sheriff hopped into his squad car and got on the horn. He spoke with the dispatcher and made a call to the nearest military base, Ft. Campbell. After the deputies were up to speed, Antione applied a tourniquet to Lomax's injured legs and tried to stop the blood from gushing from his mangled arm and lacerated stomach. He couldn't, no matter how much he tried, stop Lomax from slipping into a state of shock. The deputies gave Antione a hand keeping their injured colleague warm, by wrapping him within a few police blankets.

Lomax was shaking like a leaf in the wind. He was sweating profusely but was cold to the touch. After taking a quick look around, the sheriff decided that it would be best to get out of the wooded areas. Lomax needed immediate medical attention. The military had suggested that he be quarantined until their arrival. The sheriff wouldn't wait to get him some medical help. No one had really taken the time to investigate the severely mauled areas of Lomax's anatomy, so no one noticed that those areas were regenerating by themselves.

***

The passengers of *The Aquaticus* were excited. The Video-cam lines were almost overloaded with calls between the passengers. The captain, somewhat surprised by the information, kept his course steady and true. His mind was, however far away from the present.

***

The creatures collected their injured and fallen members and swarmed back into the hive for immediate departure. The hive rippled as the creatures went inside. The hive's shape changed. It flattened out along the sides, the front sharpened to a point, and the swollen end extended some sort of ovular tail fin. The hive then silently hovered above the creek bed. The front end of the hive pointed toward the clear blue sky, and within the blink of an eye, it was no more.

***

Mr. Lakur was monitoring the VC interactions with excitement. This moment was even more exhilarating than he'd thought it would be. The passengers were conversing with one another and becoming aware of their commonalities. The dreams or visions they exchanged knowledge of, clarified the long, confusing mystery in which they all portrayed some role.

***

The military team from Ft. Campbell arrived in the Dayton marshland at fifteen hundred hours. They quarantined the town. Using military hover backs and hydrofoils, they combed and surveyed every inch for four square miles. The river where everything had started showed no sign of the oddly described creatures, which had supposedly taken the poor town by surprise.

The whole town was accounted for except for a few elderly townspeople. The military closed off every possible route for departure from the town. The creeks were blockaded; MP's patrolled the roads with live ammo. There was no trace of anything out of the ordinary.

***

UKNI-net's massive intelligence kept its millions of sensors and eyes focused on the blue globe above which it hung. Monitoring the billions of military and civilian transmissions, she kept vigilant order within the constant threat of chaos. She also watched the curious little blue bubble closely. Even from the distance of five hundred miles above the Earth's atmosphere, she examined it with extreme prejudice.

Her electronic eyes continually scanned each section of the object for something familiar. Nuclear powered lasers assisted in the examination of the object centimeter by centimeter. Electromagnetic scans reached deep into the orb-like object, monitoring the trans-mutagenic substance and the biologicals within for a simple, common, polypeptide, or hydrocarbon combination. She found one compound that was common on Earth.

The creatures had a large amount of C_6H_6. She made no diagnosis; she simply compiled her minor findings and transmitted the information to the military scientists gathered at Cape Kennedy.

Chapter 22

The day was sunny and clear as *The Aquaticus* cleared the final ten miles at a leisurely 2 knots per hour. The swallows were riding the invisible roller-coaster-like currents of air with wings outstretched. Within three miles of the destination, there was a crack of thunder that shook *The Aquaticus*. *The Aquaticus* was suddenly engulfed in a myriad of dark clouds, and the sea's cool hand reached back and forth across the deck for any unsuspecting soul it could drag down into its dark blue depths.

After recovering, the captain sounded the alert siren. Everyone was required to get to the nearest hatch and get inside. The crew responded quickly, ushering the passengers below deck as the crew made their way to various designated positions along the deck. Close computer monitoring notified the captain when everyone was safely sealed inside cabins or safe areas on the boat. He tapped a button on the control panel, swiftly but silently encasing the ship in a protective coating of titanium-enriched steel that gave it the appearance of a large white bullet. The captains' computer was now insulated from magnetic interference caused by the storm.

Once the rough, tossing and turning of the

sea subsided to a more tolerable level the shielding was dropped, allowing passengers and crew to rush outside and see what was left of the storm that had struck so violently.

***

The hive was gliding within a pre-existing cloud. The cloud's droplets of water gave the perfect camouflage for the hive. Since the instruments UKNI-Net used to scan the clouds worked on the basic bouncing of radio waves, the trillions of miniature signals produced by the water droplets kept the hives position shrouded.

***

Lomax was coming out of his state of shock, but something was not right. He wasn't cringing in pain or screaming like a baby. The soldiers were standing around with their mouths hanging dryly open. He stood up, looked around at the soldiers and walked toward the sheriff.

The sheriff stared in awe as Lomax walked toward him without as much as a small limp. No explanation could have helped ease the sheriff's troubled state. The infantrymen of the military team were all dumbstruck. The C.O. of the squadron called for Lomax to be brought back into the quarantine vessel for additional testing.

Lomax, vaguely recalling what had happened, began to examine himself. His minds sharpness fought with the fuzzy images his memory was spewing forth. He could feel that his legs were ok except for some patches of skin. The skin wasn't soft and pliable like it was supposed to be but was hard to the touch. He also felt his right arm that had been almost taken off by the bite of the things that attacked him. He began to panic as his mind began to behave strangely. He started to have flashbacks of memories that weren't his. A hunger arose inside him, but hunger for what; he had no clue.

***

The C-17 transport was about to take off when its departure request was recalled. The pilots were told to stand down and await additional cargo. Pissed off, but obedient, they drove their plane back to the hanger and hopped out to get a couple of soft drinks for the flight.

The scientists at Ft. Blunts 101st airborne in Tennessee were brilliant. They created miniature-self-imploding missiles with a compact mercury impact detonation tip. The weapons triggered on impact and would release a large electrical current through the titanium shell of the missile causing it to become red hot.

They hoped with all their skills and technical know-how that this device could quite possibly help to save the world. Upon the mass production of these little missiles, which they adapted to the bio-metal interfacing mechanisms of the SQUADS uniforms, they sent the first shipment of two thousand rounds to the team's transport and issued forth the clearance for departure.

The SQUADS equipment was then loaded onto the fully fueled C-17 plane. The plane was also loaded with four new prototype vehicles. Each one had enough room for up to four individuals and whatever armaments they would have to carry. The prototypes were marked with the initials of APLR-1 thru 4.

The pilots were looking at the manuals for the weird looking vehicles. Apparently, these were the first real all-terrain vehicles. The abbreviations stood for Air-Phibious Land-Rovers. They could be used in ground and air assaults, as well as in nautical maneuvers. They had vertical lift off like a harrier jet but were more efficient in acceleration and with fuel consumption. They had no seams where the metal was welded together, nor any glass for vision, so they assumed that the vehicles were equipped with highly sensitive electronics.

***

The port side of the ship held a clear sky and calm ocean, which was just a little peculiar, considering the violent storm that had hit *The Aquaticus*. The starboard view kept most of the passengers flabbergasted.

"My God," Julius Canton Sr and his wife Maudine said in unison.

There were collective sighs and gasps from other passengers on board as they stood along the deck taking in the view. There was the island that they had all seen before only in dreams and most recently in video form. Pure white sand, lush eucalyptus trees, palm trees and fruit trees of all kind.

"It's real, it's really a real place," Charles said as he wrung his hands.

Lana and Lameka where standing alongside Charles. Tears were streaming down their faces. Lameka said in a hushed tone, "I can't believe it, we're really here."

As *The Aquaticus* reached its closest approach point, many of the passengers made their way to the deck to take in the view. Many of the newly surfaced passengers stood pointing and gasping. A few fell to their knees, overcome by the pure emotion of the moment. The captain issued the command for the crew to drop anchor and secure an area on the beach for shore investigations. The beachhead team piled into the shuttle boat and headed for the beautiful white sands of the beach. Pine and eucalyptus fragrances beckoned the helmsman of the shuttles. Two vessels left *The Aquaticus* for re-con and security measures before the passengers would be allowed to go ashore.

A few members of *The Aquaticus'* security crew departed from the secured deck toward the beach on a separate boat.

The Lakur industry was known for tight security detailed uniforms and optical devices, so each man was armed with a semi-automatic 7mm miniature grenade-launching rifle and was equipped with two min-cam's wired into their helmets and their uniform collars.

The uniforms were lightweight Kevlar and rather comfortable for the jungle reconnaissance they were being used for. The first schooner from *The Aquaticus'* perch reached the shore. The team secured their landing site and proceeded with an excursion into the foliage.

The captain was called into the Lakur suite. As he journeyed down the hatchways toward his destination, he could do nothing to stop his mind from spinning. The island in all its precious beauty held something secret deep within its heart. As he reached the suite Lakur was opening the door. Lakur motioned for the captain to follow him back through a barrage of passageways he'd known nothing about before this moment. The captain's mind was bombarded with questions he didn't ask.

Soon they reached a hall that he recognized by its markings as an entrance to the other half of the storage bay that held all of the concealed equipment boxes. There was a doorway with an electronic hand imprint sequencer placed around the upper three-quarter mark of the door.

Lakur firmly but gently placed his hand onto the sequencer. The doorway made a hissing noise, then a slight rumble before it retreated into the wall. The captain just stood there, watching and waiting until the hissing stopped. There was a murky blackness that stood where the doorway had been. The mechanical scent of the air was overpowered by a strong antiseptic odor.

Lakur stepped into the darkness without hesitation; however, the captain did not follow. Waiting at the doorway, he heard the faint squeaking sound of Lakur's cross trainers fading as he moved further into the darkness. A few moments later the lights came on in the room.

"I'm sorry captain, please come inside," Lakur stated rather calmly.

As the captain entered the room, the first thing that caught his attention was a self-contained, transparent eight-foot tall environmental storage chamber that took up over half of the storage rooms space. Lakur came from behind the chamber with two computerized backpacks.

He handed one to the captain with the explanation, "As you've recently found out, this voyage is, well I guess you could say, scientific. For many years, these people, the members of the crew, you, and even I, have been trying to find answers to many questions that have plagued our every waking moment. Over the years, I've done my homework, and many things have become apparent to me. One of which is this peculiar island that we've found. This island has been drawn and described by many of the passengers on this vessel, years before my experimental team discovered its existence."

The captain quietly stood there soaking in this information. His facial expression was stoic, but his mind raced, trying to find out what his role was going to be in all of this.

Lakur continued excitedly "This island defies the laws of nature, gravity and inertia. It appears, overtly, to be a natural formation, but upon closer observation, it simply doesn't fit. It doesn't appear on any map that has been generated by the various mapping companies because apparently, our satellites have been unable to infiltrate this island's electromagnetic-camouflaging capabilities."

The captain sat down on a stool along the wall next to a workbench as he continued listening to Mr. Lakur.

Continuing Lakur stated, "Now, what I believe is that this island has been imprinted for some reason into our minds. While you, yourself, have not reported the visions of this island, you have in the past - according to psych reports, been noted to refer to an underwater tunnel."

At the mention of the tunnel, the captain's eyes widened in curiosity as he thought, *the tunnel dreams, now this is starting to make sense to me.*

Lakur noticing the captain's expression change and proceeded with his oration, "Now, as I understand it, your family is rooted in the southeastern area of Tennessee. You, having been the only child, received the best of everything your parents could afford. However, none of that seemed to be enough for you. Even as a young man, you've always seemed to be motivated by something other than material things, otherwise you'd still be in the military. I also noticed your medical history is barely short of superb. Never a broken bone; never a common cold: no chicken pox or any other common childhood illness. That, my dear captain, I find very intriguing."

"Mr. Lakur, I'm not sure what is so intriguing, I've always been very healthy." The captain responded.

"I'm getting to that. You see my dear captain; I don't know your particular part in all this as of yet. What I do know is that you are a part of it, just as every individual on this boat is, and coming to this island at this time, I believe will help us all understand what is going on." Lakur said with a smile.

Adair Rowan

Chapter 23

The Lakur security team fanned out to about five yards between each member and began a slow and extremely cautious journey into the foliage. Within less than thirty feet they knew something didn't seem normal in this place, and it wasn't just their imaginations.

The sense of Déjà vu was powerful among them. They looked closely at the trees and plant life around them, a few quickly formulating a hypothesis. The island wasn't natural. The trees were covered with a skin that resembled an iguana's frumpy looking flesh. There were no signs of deterioration, mushrooms or lichen present in the sand-like terrain they were working their way through. In fact, even the sand felt strange. It didn't merely shift around the impact point. It actually seemed to get firmer and hold its position better than compacted dirt. The team members made a note of this and took pictures of the forestry before proceeding further, deeper, into the unknown.

The forest was made up of the most peculiar combination of plants. Fica and ferns, pine resembling greenery, all types of bushes and shrubbery. There were a few trees, spaced out here and there, which had the scaly appearance to them.

The bark of the tree looked reptilian. There were a few patches of discoloration that deviated from the general appearance of the trees, but nothing more. Nelson, one of the male security team members, took extensive pictures of the trees while noting the peculiar absence of insects.

He stopped the team so they could take environmental samples for the return trip. As he knelt in the rubbery sand-like soil; he pulled out the sample container when an eerie glow descended on the team.

Nelson slowly turned to track the origin of the glow and froze. Floating above the team, the most amazing, fluorescent, orb-shaped object took his breath away. Instinctively reacting, he reached to unclasp the lock on his shoulder holster. Slowly, he gripped the cool handle of his pearl-handled, chrome Beretta, pulled it out and took aim at the orb.

Everyone else in the team had already pulled their weapons, but no one pulled a trigger. The orb had descended and was now resting at chest level directly in the center of the team's circle. No one wanted to empty a round into a fellow team member accidentally, so they all stood staring at the orb.

The team's initial reaction was due to its strangeness, but none of the group felt any real alarm. The orb extended pseudopodia of whimsy, vaguely transparent gas, which slowly crept out and touched the tense minds of the group. Images flashed of the trees and blotchy areas. No one understood, but they knew instinctively that there was no harm intended.

They put away their weapons and observed as the orb ascended to the overhanging tree limb toward a blotchy spot. The gaseous tendril was re-extended toward a discolored area of the tree and began to siphon away the discoloration. It moved from tree limb to tree limb siphoning the blotches until it was almost five times its original size. At this point it again sent images to the team, depicting the pathway they should take to get where they needed to go.

A golden streak formed on the underbelly of the orb creature, which uncannily resembled a directional arrow. The team, taking this as a sign, followed the orb through the shrubs and bushes as it seemed to be clearing a path about ten feet ahead of each member's next step.

In a surprised tone, one of the female team members said aloud, "Are you seeing this?"

The rest of the team responded in a chorus, "Yes, we are."

Nelson dropped magnetic markers every hundred or so steps, as they moved along at a brisk pace. They came upon a clearing which bordered a small lake. What caught their attention was the smaller island that perched in the middle of the lake.

Details from the eye level area of the inner island were obscured due to a thick mist that draped around its base. The orb continued on above the water without disturbing the surface, until it occasionally dipped and arced to contact the surface of the water somewhat playfully as it proceeded toward the inner island.

Nelson pulled on his binoculars and watched the buoyant dance of the orb along its path. He put down the binoculars, whipped out the beta-cam and filmed the orbs procession until it disappeared into the mist; which concealed most of the inner island from view. Unable to calculate the islands complete size, he sat down to soak in the sight.

The team stood, as one, for a few moments in wonderment. They took pictures using various types of film, infra-red, chromo color, and even electromagnetic to get a composite shot. Leaving a magnetic marker on the shore, they turned and started back toward their landing site.

***

Groggy and stiff from their hyper induced sleep, the SQUAD, awakened in their frosty bio-compartments. Stretching to relieve stiffness and taut muscles, the SQUAD began Kata exercises. Commander Edwards led them through the twenty-minute workout. Once completed, they sat down at the virtual data ports and linked up with UKNI-NET.

The information about the APLR assault crafts poured into their heightened minds at an astounding rate. The new vehicles were streamlined for speed and armed for destruction including a compliment of 50, acidic-bio-cast armor-piercing missiles each. They were more prepared for battle than any branch of the military. The four APLR's rested in the cargo bay of the C-17 like king cobras waiting for the right moment to strike at unsuspecting prey.

The four-passenger assault crafts had no visible opening in the quantum flux bio-armor; which was designed to communicate with the Squads TA-3 uniforms. Also polymorphic in nature, the vehicles could assume almost any outward appearance of the same size and volume. The twenty-mile notice light glowed throughout the cargo compartment as the SQUAD dissolved into their vehicles.

***

The hive hovered within the eye of a waterspout that sprung up on a group of unsuspecting fishermen. The fishermen were moving back and forth trying to secure mooring and rigging, pulling the net in as fast as possible. The captain had already upshifted the engine and was trying to steer clear of the spout as quickly as possible.

The hive noticed the crude vessel, including its passengers and began to descend down through the center of the waterspout. Ta-Laun, a rather buffed young deckhand noticed the dark area that appeared in the neck of the waterspout and drew attention to it. As the dark area moved down the spout the crew watched in silence. The captain rang the alert bell when he noticed that the net hadn't been secured. The startled crew frantically resumed their work, occasionally glancing up as they tracked the darkness reaching the bottom of the spout before disappearing under the swirling foam of sea water.

When they realized that there was no impending danger, the crew settled back into their work. They finished securing all the mooring and went below deck for sandwiches and drinks.

Ta-Laun sat on the fish deck, resting with his back against a tightly wound stack of heavy-duty rope. He pulled out a piece of mango and bit into the succulent fruit. The juice cooled his salt-air dried throat. He closed his eyes and allowed his body to feel the ocean rhythm. He tried to take a short nap, but the boat's engine was too loud. He was only able to relax enough to ease the crooks from his tense neck muscles. Just as he got awkwardly comfortable, there was an unusual thumping sound that resounded throughout the hull of the vessel.

Startled from his already non-existent doze, Ta-Laun sprang up to investigate. The hair on the back of his neck stood on end, his gut churned and goose bumps ran up and down his spine. He picked up a compact spear turret from underneath a deck board near the railing of the ship.

He glanced over the starboard rail and saw

nothing, but he still had an uneasy feeling. He began to search the exterior of the boat section by section. Slowly he crept along the deck, senses pushed to the edge in anticipation, nerves taut, and reflexes ready. As he got closer to the steering compartment, he grabbed a flare gun from the emergency locker located just outside the main cabin hinge. Just as he loaded the flare ammo into his left pocket, he heard a muffled crunching sound. Then there was a wet thrashing noise and an odd sounding thud within the cabin. His heart dropped as his mind raced with possibilities. *Have we been boarded by pirates?*

Ta-Laun squatted under the window of the cabin and glanced over the ledge. What he saw stopped his breathing. There it was, his worst nightmare: a dull, dark, gray-black figure with a face full of teeth loomed in a crouched stance. The body of the creature was covered with a shell-like body armor. It was gnawing on the remains of one his shipmates.

With no head, Ta-Laun could only guess at the identity of the victim. The mutilated remains sat slouched against the wall, oozing blood and other fluids from the open neck and gouged chest. The creature's full attention was focused on gorging itself on its prey.

Appalled and consumed with anger, Ta-Laun threw open the cabin door and unloaded several shots from his CST and then reached for the flare gun. The spears from his weapon, razor sharp, pierced the armor of the beast and pinned it to the inner cabin wall. It let out a screech that sent Ta-Laun dashing back out of the cabin toward the aft deck of the schooner.

He could hear the creature behind him as it ripped itself free from the paneling. It screeched again in what Ta-Laun could only assume was pain. Unloading the flare pistol, he glanced back as the creature stuck its head and torso out of the doorway. Teeth were all that he could distinctly make out. There were dull, glowing spaces spaced at even intervals along what was obviously the monsters head. Maybe these were the eyes of the beast.

Running out of maneuverable space, Ta-Laun felt that it was time to stand his ground. The creature was coming down the hallway in his direction quickly. It moved like a spider on its segmented legs. Stealthily, it progressed like a silent bullet train. Ta-Laun took aim and pulled the trigger. The flare hit the midsection of the monstrosity and stopped it in its tracks, but only for a second or two. The entry point smoldered, and the beast clawed at it and then resumed its attack run.

Ta-Laun loaded another flare into the flare gun and dived toward a large pile of fishing nets. Rolling on his side, he aimed at the creature's head. With accidental precision, he hit the creature in the middle of a bulbous region that amassed over a third of the creature's cranium. The creature stopped dead in its tracks. Ta-Laun cleared his chamber and loaded another flare.

The monster remained still for a moment before it began shaking uncontrollably. The body of the creature smoldered before emitting dark smoke. The thick, rancid cloud soon wafted in Ta-Launs direction.

It smelled as if someone had poured gasoline on a stack of sulfur and lit a match. The body collapsed as it slowly lost the battle against the conquering flames. Ta-Laun grabbed a CO_2 extinguisher and put the stinking, slimy corpse out before the flames could ignite the rest of the boat. Once finished he quickly searched the entire boat hoping to find other survivors. He hoped that he wouldn't run into any more of the creatures. Luck was on his side because the hive was almost twenty miles away from the boat by the time he had killed the stowaway.

Adair Rowan

Chapter 24

Nelson was excited by what he and his team had witnessed. He kept playing the sequence of events over and over in his mind as he radioed *The Aquaticus* to notify everyone that they had secured the area. He thought about how the gaseous creature only observed them as they were observing it. He wondered, "what is the significance of the color distorted areas on the trees which seemed to provide the orb with its energy and sustenance."

He was utterly clueless about what he was facing. He knew how to deal with terrorist, chaotic crowds, lunatics, and trained killers, but he had no experience when it came to what he had seen. He pondered, "What else will we find on this expedition?"

***

The hive caught a ride on the gentle currents of the ocean. It dived into the darkness to explore the reaches of this watery realm. Few of the hive members left the comfort of the hives protective sheath during these excursions. A couple of hive members, hunger-crazed, attacked a group of sharks. The sharks didn't have a chance as the hive members swooped in, quick and viciously. They tugged the squirming bodies of the sharks back to the hive so that the community could eat. Once they'd reduced the sharks to cartilage, the hive changed its bearings to head for the island.

***

The payload hangar door opened slowly creating a vacuum which sucked out anything that wasn't nailed down. The APLR's engines hummed to life. The Squad leaders piloted. The five, quantum armored vehicles glided forward in procession toward the open sky. The vehicles dropped from the plane for eight seconds before turning the engines up to full power.

The eight-second drop was mandatory so that the powerful jet stream the engines created didn't crush other vehicles close by. The vehicles sliced through the air and danced along the clouds, darting back and forth like hungry gnats cleaning the bones of a dead animal.

Commander Edwards and The Squad members admired the agility of the crafts. Edwards thought to himself during their flight, *the technology used to make these vehicles isn't from Earth. But, who the hell cares, as long as these vehicles are able to help the Squad defeat whatever we are about to face.*

***

Lomax began having visions of an island, there in his holding cell. In his mind, he concluded that he wasn't daydreaming. It was as though someone was transmitting the image into his brain. He was unsure what it meant, only that he had to get there, and very soon.

***

The passengers on *The Aquaticus* packed up their diving gear and took every available boat, to rush ashore. Stepping upon the shore, they were all mesmerized by the feel of the island. Many had a sense of having been there before, not physically, but in a voyage of their minds. They knew somehow that this was right. The passengers divided up into sets of six or more for their journey. Mr. Lakur lead the first group, followed by a group led by Dr. Ronaw and the last group lead by Mr. Canton.

Everyone gasped and pointed at the foliage of the island. Anticipation and curiosity fueled the groups desire to keep going. Everyone made it to the inner shore in less than an hour. These people were all from different walks of life, but they were all in great shape. There weren't any cries for a pause. Nobody complained about being tired or out of breath.

Gasps and sighs filled the air as the groups met up at the inner shore of the island. People began asking about the gaseous orb that the security team had reported seeing. Having only the tape in the beta-cam as evidence, Nelson allowed those who were insistent take a look. They were all astonished and bewildered by the ghostly apparition. Mr. Lakur was speechless for once, given his background.

The passengers wanted to take a little time to discuss what they were seeing and experiencing.

Mr. Lakur bellowed to the groups, "We are losing light, and I would hate to lose any one of you trying to press on in darkness. So, I suggest that we make camp here and pick this up in the morning."

In response to Mr. Lakur's remarks The Canton family, Julius, Maudine, Junior and Gina cleared a nice sized area on the sands of the inner shore and made camp. Each group followed suit. That night the whole entourage dined on dried fruits and canned meats. Many sat along the edge of the inner shores and stared at the smaller island off in the distance shrouded by fog. Their minds needed time to sort out the information they'd been exposed to.

Many conversations centered on the facts.
1. They all shared a common dream about a farm,
2. They all dreamed about a peculiar island, on which they now stood
3. They all had this disquieting feeling that something was coming for them but had no clue what it was.

Some sat around that night joking about what it could possibly be. Julius Jr humorously said, "Maybe it is The Thing with its ever-changing, life-form-mimicking ways, and maybe it's already in the camp feeding off of some unsuspecting soul, while taking on his or her appearance."

Gina answered back, "What if it was the devil himself; standing off in the weeds, instructing the wildlife of this little island to attack certain members of the party."

Other members in the group laughed dismissively as everyone settled in for the night.

Nelson, being wary of the welcoming surroundings, set up several photo-sensitive cameras and motion detecting devices around the campsite before turning in for sleep.

Adair Rowan

Chapter 25

The military units from Ft. Blunt doubled the men on blockade duty and then took the Sheriff, Lomax, Antione and the remaining deputies into quarantine. No one was happy about this. They put up a serious protest about the violation of their rights without cause.

The only one that didn't actually protest was Lomax. He knew, better yet, he could feel that there was a reason for him to be contained. They were all loaded into an armored security vehicle for transport back to Fort Blunt.

Upon their arrival, they were all subjected to duplicate and triplicate testing. They were poked and prodded until they were very irritable. Each of them was placed within their own five by seven unit, with security outside. The military scientists were particularly interested in the growths on Lomax's body. They subjected him to multiple MRI scans which revealed an abnormal growth in the cerebral cortex of his brain. It looked like swollen tissue, a concussion, but after further examination, the growth was traced down into the chest cavity.

As they returned Lomax to his cell, the lead Doctor could be overheard as he was leaving the holding area saying, "The weird thing about the growths in Lomax, is that they are still growing. They are increasing in size beyond the microscopic level at an enormous rate."

The scientists were attempting to analyze a small sample to figure out the composition and structure of the cells. The problem was that the cells kept dying before they could get them to an examination table.

Lomax began to feel feverish as waves of nausea gripped his insides. The soldiers outside weren't watching him, so they didn't notice that his complexion had turned ghastly pale. He faded in and out of consciousness within containment.

As his strength waned with each bout of delirium, he fell violently to the floor. At the sudden noise, the soldiers outside peeked into the cell. They were startled by what they saw. Something strange was happening to Lomax's body. It wasn't quite human anymore. It was composite of a human and possibly whatever it was that had attacked Lomax. The cranial structure was a slightly extended version of that of a human, with multiple eyes. It was a very dark shade of gray, almost the same color as the inside of the unit. The soldiers moved back from the containment unit door and called for help. Almost instantly, every alarm in the complex erupted to life, they were almost deafening. Soldiers converged on the unit from both ends of the hallway as well as the outer perimeter. As each soldier took up his position along the corridor, poised for action, they all waited. After approximately seven minutes the alarms were discontinued.

***

It was an absorbing morning. The passengers of *The Aquaticus* were up before sunlight became prominent. The area was humming with activity as they went about breaking down camp.

Nelson and the security team did a short scout of the route they took to get to the inner shore, just to be sure that the trail was still marked. Once the area was secured, the team set about the task of retrieving the load of new diving gear from the cargo bay. The task took about two hours to complete.

With everything accounted for they began assigning inflatable rafts to the groups for their journey to the interior isles shore. They all donned scuba gear and kept the tanks and flippers nearby just in case.

Lahm was enthusiastic about it all and made sure that he was on the lead raft to the next shore. You could almost feel the adrenaline pumping through all of them. It was thick like Karo syrup straight out of the refrigerator. Everyone sat quietly, soaking in their surroundings as the rafts were pushed along by compact motors. Nothing breached the surface of the water, nor was there any indication of activity of any kind on the embankment of the inner isles shore. It was peaceful except for the gentle hum of the motors.

Nelson felt a quiver tugging at his gut. Was it anticipation or anxiety? He had no words to define the feeling. He shouted out "Stop here! Everyone stopped and looked inquisitively toward Nelson. The drivers shut the power off so that the boats slowed to drift toward the inner isle.

Nobody knew what had made Nelson yell out, but everyone heeded his abrupt command. Mr. Lakur was obviously perturbed by this and acidly glared at Nelson. Not waiting for the questions, Nelson spoke, "Need I remind everyone that the dreams we've all had, involved an underwater tunnel."

Mr. Lakur's expression softened as he recognized what Nelson was talking about. Nelson continued, "In my dreams, I do not recall ever actually reaching the inner isle."

The murmurs from the rafts were ones of agreement. Mr. Lakur suggested, "Why don't we bring the rafts close enough to bind them together as one platform before deciding on the next move."

They all agreed. After the rafts were all bound, they all sat to discuss whether they should take turns diving or whether they should all dive together.

***

Final systems checks of the APLR's were in the green. The Squads APLR vehicles responded remarkably. Their strafing maneuvers were performed at undreamed velocities.

The Squad flew in an extremely tight, four-point formation.

The APLR's pierced the surface of the ocean with little splashing and began their slower nautical journey toward the uncharted island.

Their link with UKNI-Net provided them with the coordinates, which according to satellite information; showed up as a stable, unchanging void. Checking the equipment aboard the vehicles was so simple it barely took a few seconds to verify that all systems were functioning properly.

The Navi-Com systems took over as the Squad members rested. The journey would take several hours at their present speed of 30 knots an hour. During this time, the Squad received their synthesized amino rations.

Adair Rowan

Chapter 26

The C.O. of the DeCon unit reached the site within minutes of the alarm with a battery of elite martial officers. He questioned the soldiers present about what they had witnessed. Since the duty officers were the only ones that had seen anything, they were the only ones with anything to report.

The lead officer stated, "Sir, we were standing here and heard a loud thump from the cell. As we looked inside through the viewing portal, we saw what appeared to be something erupting from Lomax's body sir."

When the C.O. heard their description of what they witnessed, amusingly he responded, "What? Are you serious right now?"

Seeing that they were not believed they turned on the floodlights within the cell and told the C.O., "See for yourself sir, this is no joking matter."

He glanced into the cell, as he did so, he stiffened up and slowly turned back to the soldiers.

"Um, what the hell," The C.O. stammered, and took a second, slower glare into the unit. He was mute for few moments as he stared at the creature in the cell, that had once been deputy Lomax.

The creature glared back as its body

continued its metamorphosis. The brainpan area had expanded in an elliptical fashion and the lower jawbone had doubled in size. The appendages that used to be Lomax's legs had been discarded with the ease in which a snake sheds its skin. They had been replaced by a set of six double-sized exoskeleton covered legs. His hands had become like the claws of a crab, with powerful forearms. His torso still resembled that of a human; only it was also covered with a stiff, thick exoskeleton.

Lomax, physically, was no longer even remotely human. However, he still retained, only partially, the ability to speak. He was waving his claw toward the C.O., in a motion to come closer, which he wouldn't do. After a few moments, this thing that was once Lomax began to speak in a slow sputtering tone.

"Danger, island, must go," Lomax said. Something was wrong with the creature because its legs were trembling under its burdensome body. It collapsed against the wall of the containment unit and lay there with its legs extended in an awkward position. The C.O. ran down the corridor, followed by his martial officers, into the research locker room. Once there they searched for enclosed suits to wear into the unit.

The martial officers tugged on pressurized, bio-enhancement armor that increased their strength. With everyone equipped, they proceeded back into the cell. Seeing that the C.O. and his men were about to enter the unit, the security officers retreated back as far as they could without giving the impression that they were deserting.

The Security bolts were removed from the door and four soldiers in riot gear pulled it away from the units' entrance. With the entrance clear, the officers took up a position facing the unit with their weapons pointed at the creature.

***

In order not to waste too much time, the passengers agreed that the security team should do a brief re-con dive. Nelson and two others of his security team threw on their compression tanks and checked the gauges.

They strapped on the slender but deadly CST rifles and jumped in. The water was warm and exceptionally clear. Nelson felt, in his gut, that he was doing the right thing. His mind reached for ideas regarding what he should do next. He decided to check for radioactive contaminants in the water along with his general investigation.

The team split up and began a twenty-minute scout of the channel separating the two islands. Nelson started toward the inner island's perimeter. He was looking for the drop off point where the shore simply disappeared and became a jagged wall that extended toward the ocean floor.

One of the Security team members held his position approximately sixty feet below the joined rafts as the other man swam toward the shore that they had all come from. The security member, standing fast, made the observation that the shore from which they had come seemed to disappear once you reached a depth of one hundred feet.

He swam down and saw that it became a flat vertical wall that extended down as far as the eye could see. It filtered into the dark abyss which resided patiently below. Upon a vertical descent of some eighty or so feet, Nelson noticed that the composition of the inner isle went, gradually, from rough to smooth.

He wondered, "What natural process could have this effect?"

Reaching the other two members of his security team, he gave the ascension signal to begin heading for the rafts.

***

The martial officers surrounded the creature with a crescent maneuver. It neither stirred nor showed any signs of aggression. Its breathing was slow and very labored. The humanness of Lomax was still fighting from within the grotesque body of the creature he had become.

The martial officers took up defensive positioning close enough to the monster to let it know that if it attacked, they were prepared to respond with deadly force. The C.O. moved in as close as he dared to the creature.

He pulled out a small Digi-rec unit to record whatever transpired between the creature and himself. The creature began to speak, in an agonizing manner. Its voice was hollow as it gasped for air between its words as it made a feeble attempt to communicate with the C.O.

As it spoke, it struggled to keep clarity, "The creature I've become is a form of life which ravishes a galaxy some five light years away. The name we have cannot be translated into your language. We are very intelligent."

The struggle in the rapidly mutating human eyes was very apparent. "You should prepare your world to be conquered because there is no hope for your kind. I am a creature that is some two hundred earth years old. My kind has a genetically neutral composition; therefore, we can exist and procreate in almost any environment."

It was as if the creature was having an identity crisis. It was struggling within itself for control. What once was Lomax, a deputy sheriff, was now fighting with all of the discipline and training that had allowed him to become a law enforcement officer. He broke through every now and then during the conversation hoping to give some valuable information to the soldiers before him.

"I can tell you this sir. . . the creature is having some trouble suppressing my personality. It grew and nourished itself on my cerebral cortex, thereby making it essentially human." Lomax said.

The C.O. asked, "How do you know this?"

"It's interesting," Lomax replied as he

continued to speak during this struggle of the minds.

"Its mind and my mind work in conjunction with one another. At least for now. For it to use the knowledge that I have of this world, it has to allow its mind to be open, which allows me to glimpse into its thoughts…some of the sights that my mind has been exposed to are beyond the realm of my understanding." Lomax shrugged and gasped.

Coughing, he continued, "I must tell you the reason that they are here."

The C.O. fielded the question, "Yes, that's it, why are they here Lomax?"

There was a pause as the struggle continued before Lomax proceeded. "We are here to retrieve a race of individuals which we thought were destroyed in an intergalactic chase over twenty-five of your earth years ago. They are the most vicious and deceptive beings that our society has ever known. Genetically they are linked to us, like what you call distant cousins."

"If they've been here for twenty or so years, why have they not attacked our people?" the C.O. shot back.

"That is not for me to understand. I'm simply one of the sixty or so...enforcement officers of my people sent to find and eliminate the creatures before they attack and destroy your world." Lomax said laboriously.

The C.O. thought about what Lomax had said then countered with, "Wait a minute! If your kind is here to help us, why did you assault the officer that you presently inhabit and his company with such viciousness without first attempting to communicate with them?"

The creature fell silent for a few moments as it decided on what it was going to say. The last ounce of Lomax which was left within the creature burst forth one last time to explain, "This creature is very deceptive, and its main reason for being here is to retrieve the beings that their race tried to wipe out years ago. The secondary mission is to decide whether or not its kind should come back to Earth and use mankind as an alternate food source." Lomax said, and then collapsed into convulsions.

The security team closed in a little closer as the convulsions stopped. Lomax seemed to break through again, only to state, "The main collection of creatures like me are on their way right now to a remote and almost undetectable island off the coast of the Bermuda Islands. This island is where they were able to trace the most extensive group of the beings they are searching for."

The C.O. was taking mental notes to add to his report. Lomax arduously continued, "The very beings that they shot down over two decades ago. They simply want to round up their slaves, so to speak, and then decide whether or not the people of Earth should be treated in the same manner."

The creature's speech became garbled and almost unintelligible, as the final mutations took hold. The C.O. backed away and signaled his men to exterminate the creature. They used flamethrowers to destroy the body to prevent any contamination that might occur should the creature's kind be spread by some spore-like manner.

The building was evacuated as the martial officers prepared the building for decontamination. The structure was exposed to a series of high-intensity gamma radiation beams before being bombed with small-scale anti-matter devices. What was left of the building was sifted for any trace of the creature's neutral genetic structure. A few traces were found and stored for further research within sub-zero liquid nitrogen tanks. These were then shipped to a top-secret facility located underground in the Cumberland Plateau. The C.O. filed his official report via his remote data terminal to his superiors.

Dr. Muerte was there to sign the papers and receive the samples. He immediately began a series of tests on the DNA to figure out a way to, if possible, duplicate the creature or eradicate it. Knowing the regenerative ability, it seemed to possess, he hoped to find the key to unlock that code and make it available for military purposes. He worked diligently and tirelessly to find that key.

Chapter 27

Once Nelson and the other two security team divers were secure on board the makeshift raft platform, they told the rest of the passengers what they had seen below. Nothing they saw would suggest any danger, including the strange way the shoreline seemed to just drop off with no natural explanation.

The more details they explained, the more unnatural the whole island seemed to become.

Lakur was more interested in going ahead with the dive like everyone else. Dr. Ronaw, on the other hand, wasn't in such a rush.

Being the Psycho-therapist, Ronaw again asked, "What is so important about this place?"

Lana was the first one to answer, "It had a strange effect on me."

Dr. Ronaw found himself answering his own question, "I was drawn to the place from the first time that I saw it on the digital tape that Mr. Lakur had shown me in his home. I was drawn but for reasons that I could not explain. Blindly going along with something has never been my way, so before I take the dive, I need to find some sort of clarification."

Mr. Canton interrupted the discussion stating, "For some reason, I have this strong need to be here. I can't put my finger on it, but, since I've been here, my mind has been at peace. I've not dreamed of this island, in fact, I've had no dreams from the war. I've slept with a peace that I've never known before. This island holds something that I need. I don't know about you all, but I must do this."

His confession left Ronaw in a state of indecision. The other members of *The Aquaticus* entourage were all eyeing him. They were waiting for him to make some sort of a decision. He pondered to himself, "I guess they figured that if I, being the logical one, agreed with what they were about to do then it would be okay."

Ronaw scanned the expectant faces of the other passengers searching for some indication of the right answer. Ronaw considered the question for a while and tossed the pros and cons back and forth in his mind.

"If I go along and nothing happens to anyone, then all they'll be is disappointed, but if something terrible happens to one of these individuals, then it will weigh heavily on my mind."

In the end, he decided that he had no real reason to deny the present course of action proposed, so Ronaw agreed to the group dive.

***

UKNI-net observed the non-Earthly vessel which traveled along the deeper recesses of the Atlantic ridge slowly and almost nonchalantly progressing towards the coordinates of The Island that could not be monitored by conventional equipment.

The UKNI-mind was trying to figure out a way to break through the interference that the island used to mask itself. UKNI tried magnetic resonance imaging, radio-active signature and micro-wave graphing to no avail. The laser examination beams on the accompanying observation satellite hadn't been used. So UKNI, in a last-ditch effort to map the space that the island occupied, set her sights on that region of the Earth and activated the beams.

To UKNI's surprise and delight the beams were altered once they reached about six thousand feet above ground level. The beams seemed to curve as if they were being directed through a complex fiber-optic web. This only showed about one-fiftieth of the islands actual size.

Upon realizing what was happening, UKNI trained five more orbiting satellites on the coordinates of the island's location and began beaming away. The information that it got back was amazing. The general make-up of the island was not something that she had ever seen.

UKNI still could not locate the islands power source, but what she was able to glean, she began transmitting to the Omega Squad which was waiting approximately six hundred miles north of the border that shielded the island. Once they received and analyzed the data, they altered their course by five degrees and reactivated the auto-pilot.

They worked on strategy during the voyage to the island, which would take another two hours at their present submerged speed. They could easily cut that in half by flying, but that would give warning to whatever it was that they were up against.

They still didn't have any real data on the creatures they might be confronting. According to mission protocol, they would not be given this information until they were past fail-safe parameters with no turning back. After a few sessions of strategy, they checked their life support links with the APLR's and took a brief nap.

***

The passengers of *The Aquaticus* checked their gear and received a briefing about diving. Dr. Ronaw pondered the possibilities over and over again in his mind. "What I would give to know what we will be facing. Will it be horrific, or will it be extraordinary?"

He checked his gear and took his place along the side of the raft-platform and waited for the signal to dive in. Lakur, Nelson and the security team were already in the water and instructing the passengers on best practices in the water. The group synchronized their diving watches so that all would be notified when it was time to resurface.

The watches also had an alert feature which would notify all the divers if the alarm was triggered by anyone who found themselves in trouble.

As the passengers descended from the rafts, they all joined hands under water until there was a full chain representing the whole group. The group then split up into smaller groups; each led by a security team member and began to swim around the base of the shoreline in search of the "cave" which had been revealed in their dreams.

Some descended a tad lower than the groups starting position and began searching along the undergrowth that had taken refuge along the ridge just before the vertical drop into darkness.

The water was very warm, extremely clear, and full of life. They spotted all types of fish and coral that most of them had never seen before. It was an educational experience for the groups.

They were underneath for almost half of an hour when all watches began buzzing. Something triggered an alert, and everyone started looking for the cause. After a few moments of confusion, one of the security team members pointed out the source.

A group member had stumbled upon a large brood of electric eels. Upon disturbing the breeding grounds, the eels began swarming out of a nearby cave in a steady stream. The entire group could have been crisp toast if the eels had considered them a threat.

The eels could have attacked but, they didn't. This was odd behavior considering that their breeding ground had been infringed upon and eels are very territorial. Once the initial excitement of finding the eel nest died down, everyone turned their attention back to finding the cave.

Time moved slowly. There was nervous energy in the water as everyone was enthusiastic about the dive and its possibilities. The find of the century was awarded to one of the members of the security team. He found what, upon first glance, looked like a shallow cave enshrouded by the expanse of an overgrown kelp bed.

Everyone in the party worked to clear away the kelp. Once the kelp was removed, tethers were attached to everyone except the security team, so that all the passengers would remain connected as they traveled through the tunnel. They could see light in the tunnel, but it wasn't very bright. The light was reflecting softly from the walls of the tunnel.

The party swam a good distance down the passageway before they could see the light directly. Judging from the distance, it would be a slightly longer swim before they would actually reach the light ahead.

Chapter 28

Dr. Ronaw thought to himself, "it appears that we are swimming along a circular arc." The farther they swam, the brighter the light was. Lakur and Nelson were in front of Ronaw, Lakur was also tethered to the group. About a quarter of the way from the light there was an odd-looking ridge that ran completely around the tunnel.

The group paused along the ridge and examined it rather closely with hydro-lights. It wasn't made of rock or coral. It was fleshy to the touch and seemed to be pulsing at a very high rate. It didn't react to being touched. Where-ever it was touched, it simply shifted back to its original shape. It felt like silly putty, gooey yet firm.

One of the security team divers pulled out a grease pencil and board, writing that it reminded them of the surface sand of the island. Ronaw nodded in agreement and made a mental note of this for later discussion. After everyone examined and touched the ridge, the group resumed their journey toward the light.

As the entire group passed through the ridged circle, they could feel the vibrations pick up in intensity. The sound amplified through the water was almost deafening. The earplugs everyone wore, were good for keeping out some water but not that sound.

For a few moments, the tunnel resonated with the vibrations and then the ridge seemed to grow. It extended itself from its resting place along the perimeter of the tunnel until it had completely cut off the tunnel in the direction from which they'd come. In response, one of the security team swam back to what was now a wall and examined it closely.

No one noticed that the fleshy, membranous ridge was full of little pockets, and from these pockets oozed a slightly blue substance before. Seeing the blue substance now, the passengers and security team swam away from the wall. They swam lower along the floor of the tunnel, as close as they could possibly swim. They picked up the pace, hurrying toward the light with more urgency.

As they swam along to the rhythmic vibrations, the blue substance that had been oozing from the wall's surface began to overtake them. It was translucent. It darkened their pathway as it surrounded the convoy, but everyone kept on swimming toward the light ahead.

Ronaw began to swim hurriedly along when he noticed that the oozing substance reacted as if it was sentient. It solidified to some degree making their ability to swim almost impossible. They were still able to move, but the effort wasn't very rewarding. Only able to turn their body in place, the group members began to look around to determine if there was a reason to be alarmed.

Ronaw was trying to focus on one of the other passengers when the tunnelway became oppressively dark. He turned back toward the way they were headed and noticed that the bright light the group had been swimming toward was almost nonexistent.

Ronaw said a mental prayer as he swam along, "Father, with all thy power and grace, please protect them, for they know not what they do. Lord, I beg of thee to cradle them within your powerful hands right now, and if it is my time to go, take me and allow them some way to keep on going."

Just as he finished the prayer, he was all but blind. Suddenly, the light at the end of the tunnel flooded the corridor. As his eyes adjusted, he glanced around for the other passengers. The liquid around him was still slightly tinted with the blue substance, but it wasn't as restrictive to his effort anymore.

***

Ronaw's first thought as he looked around was, "My eyes are getting worse."
The creatures who were now bound to him weren't the passengers that he had come with. Just about all of the passengers had been replaced by these

creatures. Gelatinous is the only word that bounced around his mind to describe them.

Only Ronaw and a few members of the security team were the only ones that were still human.

As the light revealed more of the tunnel, the creatures tethered to him began to glow more and more, as if they were absorbing the light's energy. He tugged at the cord that connected him to the group, trying to free himself if they were hostile. The security members were attempting to do so as well.

Before they could break free, Ronaw felt something tap on his shoulder. As he turned, he looked in the face of a creature, that was in the space previously held by Lakur, but it had an almost transparent body.

It had a humanoid appearance in shape, but not in substance. It waved and performed a few motions which he eventually understood as a message not to untie himself. The creature moved from him to the security members with ease and fluidity.

After the remaining humans acknowledged the message, more of the creatures began to flow in from the light, increasing the feeling of uncertainty. The new influx of creatures moved toward the ones who were still attached to the convoy cord, and there was some type of exchange. After the exchange, the creatures connected to the tethered humans simply slid free.

Ronaw was watching all of this in astonishment. Their bodies constricted until they were able to move without hindrance. It was like watching living play-doh. At this point, Ronaw began to reassess the situation. The formerly tethered creatures grabbed hold of the remaining humans and began to pull them toward the light ahead.

Ronaw thought to himself, "My greatest fear about contact with another life form has not been whether or not they would kill humans. I am more concerned about the method they would utilize."

He continued to ponder, "Would we end up like a charbroiled T-bone steak, providing the sustenance for their survival? Would they simply eat us alive, biting off chunks of our flesh as they passed through the room, watching as we struggled and cried out in constant agony until shock set in? Well, we are in it now, so we have to see it through."

The closer he and the other humans progressed toward the light, the faster his heart raced. The light wasn't just a light. It was if it had its own conscious because it dimmed as they passed through it. Upon passing through, he was able to see what looked like giant nerve cells, as his eyes adjusted. There were a few of these clusters that they were steered clear of.

As they swam through the luminescent bulbous growths, those that were transformed into this strange form of life began to glow more brightly. Ronaw was excited, as well as petrified.

He never believed that something like this could happen. The entire group exited the enormous spherical region and began to ascend. He could feel the difference in the water pressure. They were slowly rising toward a second light; however, this light wasn't blinding. As Ronaw reached the surface of the water and broke through into breathable air, he was stunned at the sight before him.

Chapter 29

The tunnel they had come through terminated within a vast underground cavern. Ronaw pulled himself from the water, just ahead of the remaining security teams breaching of the surface, and quickly made a beeline to shore so that he could take a look around. He hurriedly assisted them ashore and, alongside them, removed his surf-link diving gear.

The room was illuminated by several formations protruding from the cavern's floor. The walls within the cavern were coated with a rubbery, phosphorescent gel which seemed to be moving. There was some organization to the patterns of light it was emitting. The entire cavern was divided into sections.

There were many huge, free-standing seashell-shaped organisms within the caverns. Writhing, their insides sloshed around as if the objects were filled with some type of liquid. The security team kept busy by filming the cavern and taking photographs of everything. Ronaw stood next to one of the freestanding objects to help give some dimension to the photograph.

Touching the protrusion, Ronaw said with surprise, "It's warm, not warm enough to burn, but definitely warm."

Just as he pulled his hand away, the objects inside grew progressively dim as if someone was reducing the oxygen to a flame. It became a translucent stone gray, and a seam began to form down the center. It began to open, slowly like a Venus Flytrap. As it opened, a jelly-like liquid oozed out giving the air a slightly musky forest odor. Ronaw and the remaining security team stood around watching, recording, and taking more photos.

Like a flower petal, the flap folded itself completely down. Ronaw and the team were all silent as they watched. Lakur stepped from the opening, naked as a jaybird.

Nelson exclaimed, "What just happened!" as he backed up from the naked Lakur.

Lakur had a smile on his face. As he stepped free of the cocoon, it sealed itself and resumed its previous activity. The floor next to where Lakur stood, parted to reveal the diving gear that he had worn on the dive.

Ronaw numbly said, "What in the world?"

Lakur proceeded to put his gear on, he zipped up the torso region of the uniform, while sitting on what appeared to be a rock and smiled.

Ronaw was astonished as he absently sputtered, "I saw you disappear, you were transformed into an, I don't know what you changed into, and now, here you are."

Lakur looked like nothing was wrong, in fact, he looked jovial. He looked as if he was about to speak when the ground moved. The team and Ronaw responded by trying to find a stable rock to stand on.

More cocoons emerged from the ground. Almost a dozen pods were sliding up as if they were attached to some type of hydraulic system. As they came up, the ground directly in front of each one parted to reveal a diving uniform and surf-link gear. The people who had dived with them, who had all disappeared over an hour ago began to come forth from the cocoons.

While the passengers were emerging, the security team searched around the rest of the cavern. Everyone remained silent until the entire diving party was accounted for.

The soft musky odor which wafted around the cavern was very pungent by now. Ronaw watched in wonder as the team took a head count.

The gelatinous substance along the walls displayed images which were a tad out of focus. Ronaw still didn't understand it all.

Lakur finally began to speak, "My God Ronaw, where do I start?"

Ronaw approached him cautiously, "Pick a point, any point Lakur, I wouldn't know where to begin."

The security team gathered around closer as Lakur continued, "I now understand. I'm not, we're not, human."

The original diving members were all there now, restored to their human appearance.

"Well, I've sort of figured that out, but what exactly are all of you?" Ronaw countered while waving his hand toward the group.

Lakur in response continued, "We are called the Trigener', a race from a galaxy a few light years away."

"Trigener'?" Ronaw repeated.

Lakur answered, "Please let me explain. We, the Trigener', lived a peaceful and symbiotic existence with nature on our home world. Everything we needed, nature provided and everything we discarded, what you call "trash," lower life forms in our ecosystem used. We had the optimal symbiotic civilization."

"I see... please proceed," Ronaw said as he absorbed the story.

"We used biologic computers, some examples are here in this space around you. We didn't pollute our world like humans have done here on Earth. We were once a great society."

"Great how? Like the Egyptian or Mayan civilizations?" Ronaw asked.

"Oh! We were much, much more." Lakur said as he continued with a smile. "We have a limited telepathic ability, which allowed us to eliminate war on our world totally. We felt that all life had a purpose and that if destroyed for foolish reasons like war, that life may not reach its full potential. We felt that any life destroyed frivolously could prove to be tragic and detrimental to future generations."

Lakur paused for a moment like he was giving Ronaw time to process. Ronaw stood up and paced back and forth. After a few cycles, he turned to Lakur and said, "I'm somewhat perplexed. It seems to me, if I understand this correctly; your people had the perfect world. A world in which one could have unlimited potential for intelligence and creativity."

Lakur interjected, "Yes. A world of great artistry, music, and scientific advancement. We moved out into space to see what else was out there. Some areas of our science were based entirely on the manipulation of matter, so we traveled the stars and gathered information on dozens of other solar systems within our own galaxy.

"Your people traveled the stars?" Ronaw asked in hushed tones.

Lakur proceeded, "Yes, but, for knowledge only. We took the extra precaution of not disturbing the natural development of other worlds and civilizations that held intelligent life."

Nelson, sidling up next to Ronaw retorted, "So how did you end up here, on Earth?"

Lakur carried forward with "We arrived here on Earth due to an unfortunate turn of events.

Ronaw chimed in, "What do you mean by unfortunate?"

"Our world was attacked and utterly decimated by a race of creatures who were extremely vile and hostile. In our efforts to escape our attackers, this vessel was injured and needed a place to recover. In a last-ditch effort to escape, some of us - those standing here, were released in transformative pods similar to those we just exited from. Our ship came to rest here with the remaining crew that you met in the tunnels. Those of us who escaped via the pods used a long-term memory suppression procedure developed by our people; to hide those memories, which allowed us time to acclimate to the human life experience. This is how we have been able to live among you all of this time with little attention." Lakur explained.

Nelson interjected again, "No way! You're saying that this cave, the tunnels and all of this is a space ship?"

Lakur stood up, smiled and said, "Well, yes; yes, it is..."

Ronaw gasped, as did Nelson and the security team.

Lakur did not wait, he continued telling their story, "The vehicle that we used to get here was and is biological. This creature, our vessel is called a Steorscip."

Ronaw threw his hand up and said, "Wait a minute Lakur, did you say a biological vessel?"

"That's exactly what I said, the Steorscips were designed over thousands of years ago. They were genetically edited until they reached their current form. They can digest matter and convert it into anti-matter which they use for stellar propulsion. Their inner cavernous bodies, one of which we now stand inside of, are able to support life forms of many kinds. They have the ability to seal off areas within their bodies, to accommodate extremely different physical environments." Lakur explained.

Adair Rowan

Chapter 30

The displays along the walls of the caverns changed and began to play a sequence of moving images supporting Lakur's narrative.

"Within a cold, dark matter clouded arm of their galaxy's parent galaxy lived a race of creatures called the Charcomanti. They attacked, destroyed, and enslaved worlds for the advancement of their own race. On many of the worlds, they annihilated the higher lifeforms, with no attempt of co-habitation. The Charcomanti demonstrate no compassion or tolerance for any other race of being that they encounter. Once they controlled many of the solar systems within the spiral arm their solar system rested, they began to attack our minor galaxy." Lakur explained.

"We the Trigener' are a peaceful race who had little use for weapons of mass destruction. Neither were many of the other races that we encountered as our race moved out into the stars. Even those who were initially apprehensive, we learned to communicate with and live alongside. Most intelligent species are curious; and willing to take a chance and learn about those unfamiliar to their existence."

Ronaw interrupted again to ask, "Tell me more about this vessel we're in Lakur. You say it's alive? It's intelligent?"

Lakur transitioned, "Well, the Steorscips are living intelligent creatures, with an innate ability to control their internal structures, and they have limited telepathic ability."

"Wait, so you're saying this ship, it... it can read our minds?" Nelson stammered.

"It can but only slightly," Lakur responded.

"What does that mean?" Ronaw asked sternly.

"It means that the vessel can read general things about you, hunger, fear, happiness. More complex needs are learned over long-term exposure to your race," continued Lakur.

"Oh, so it cannot control us?" Nelson inserted.

"Right, it cannot control you," Lakur said with a smirk.

***

The finish of the Steorscip's floor seemed to resemble mother-of-pearl. Slightly translucent, one could visibly make out the pathway that the group swam through to reach the gelatinous orb that was apparently the heart and mind of this creature. There were clear divisions along the innards of the Steorscip, which determined what happened and where.

Lakur continued his exposition, "The area we occupy is the equivalent of the bridge or main control area of the Steorscip. The viewing "screen" that surrounds us monitors every direction. Near the front of the bridge are two small cubby holes which control navigation."

As he spoke, two podium-like protrusions rose from the vessels floor on either side of him.

Lakur explained them, "These are the tactical and sensor consoles."

Ronaw moved closer to examine the consoles. He cautiously began to press on the bulbous regions to see what would happen. At first, nothing happened. Then, as his palm brushed across a lightly fuzzy region on the podium, the floor directly in front of it opened to a two-inch thin gelatinous column that extended up from the floor and spread open like the back on a threatening cobra. As it solidified slightly into an ovular shape, it began to display what eventually appeared to be the underwater landscape surrounding the island.

"The technology is astounding, a living creature with the ability to holographically project an image of its surroundings," Ronaw stated as he moved from the console closer to the display.

He moved back to the console and ran his hand along the fuzzy region again causing the display to change and show the island in detail. There was the perimeter island and all types of aquatic life that lived around and underneath it. Two long creatures were cocooned within the base of the perimeter island. Their body signatures registered as a bright yellow on the monitors.

"What are those?" Ronaw asked, pointing to the yellow highlights on the display.

Lakur moved to the console, placed his hand there, and some strange symbols appeared. As he "read" Lakur answered, "These are a set of creatures called the Velitheans."

"What is a Velithean?" Ronaw stammered.

"The Velitheans are a serpentine race of creatures found on the planet Valon 3, located in what Earth scientist call the Eagle Nebula." Lakur related.

Gina Canton interjected, "Even though the Nebula is composed of mainly supercharged gas, a few minor planetoids were found to have evolved some intelligent life-forms. These serpentine creatures were the highest evolved forms of life that existed on the largest of those planetoids. Their epidermal layers are composed of tightly packed silicate molecules which give them a protective coating almost as dense and strong as titanium, but with the sharpness of a jagged-edged diamond. The Velithians are fierce creatures and allies of the Trigener."

Lakur motioned for Gina to stop as he said to Dr. Ronaw, "Mrs. Gina is actually one of our foremost scientists; therefore, she will continue. Lakur nodded to Gina who proceeded to explain.

"During the first few years that our Steorscip spent residing within the Earth's atmosphere, it was able to recuperate rapidly from the damage incurred throughout our escape from the Charcomanti attacks. Once it was back to full functionality, it created an outer ring that now serves as what you might consider a monitoring device and storage facility. The outer isle is actually a dronelike appendage of Steorscip flesh that was shed, yet is still a part of, and responds to our vessel's nervous system. The Steorscips were able to do this as an unexpected side effect of our genetic engineering. The exact mechanics of this is still not fully understood." Gina explained.

Ronaw, standing with one hand on his jaw while resting his elbow on the other crossed arm said, "So both island structures are part of the same creature? Which, you say can traverse space! How?"

Gina proceeded, "Occasionally we were able to travel between worlds through a spatial rift that Steorscips create by compressing the distance between two points in space and figuratively speaking, stepping through a doorway to the other side. During one of those trips, we came across these beings. It took us several years to learn their language, habits, and come to an understanding of their complex society. When we were confident enough, we attempted contact. Our first attempts at contact were originally ignored because we were broadcasting the message from space. Seeing that our attempts were fruitless, we decided to send a few of our kind into the subaquatic realm of Valon 3. To which, there was an immediate response."

"What was the response?" Ronaw inquired.

"The Velitheans do not like intrusions, and they let us know by limiting our contact and keeping us at a distance with aggressive actions. It took us another earth year to convince the Velitheans that we were there peacefully, and actually, requesting their assistance. Once formal communications were established, deliberations took place, and we presented our case to the Velithean elders. After understanding our request, the elders decided that they would help by sending two of their mated warriors with us, hence the pair you see on the display. They are our secondary defense against the Charcomanti. They rest in their cocoons until they are called upon by a special signal which gives them all the information needed. They are gentle creatures, but dangerous warriors when they accept the role of guardian," Gina related.

Chapter 31

Ronaw, Nelson, and the security team exchanged astonished looks at each other in response to all that they had just learned. When the display indicated a small steady stream of greenish lights that huddled in a ridge that encompassed the inner isle.

"So, what do these greenish lights represent?" asked Ronaw,

"Those are an extremely large gathering of genetically altered Moray eels," Gina responded.

"You mean the ones that we came across during our dive?" Nelson quickly shot back.

"Yes, that same group," Gina answered

"Wait a minute, so the eels that we came across didn't attack us because they what, recognized that you all were Trigener?" Nelson inquired.

Gina clarified, "That is correct. Their intelligence has been increased exponentially, and they were able to recognize that the Trigener were within the group, which is why they did not attack. Be glad that they did not Nelson, because of our genetic tampering, they are able to kick out a stunning twenty thousand volts of electricity.

"Talk about a close call," Nelson cracked.

Gina proceeded, "The volts can be emitted at will for approximately ten-second intervals. Their scales have also been altered. Upon release, the scales can continue autonomously to shred until the energy contained within the scale is used up."

"So, like a remote-controlled drill?" Nelson asked.

"Something like that," Gina responded.

Ronaw chimed in, "So, this Steorscip seems to be very well defended according to my mental checklist. Several lines of defense, with multiple stages, a complete mobile monitoring system which can be moved very quickly, responding to telepathic instructions. With all things considered, how are the Charcomanti fierce enough to force your people into hiding?"

***

Just 3 miles outside of the target zone the Omega squad members were awakened. Immediately, they ran systems diagnostics, checked the sensor logs for anomalies, and only noted one. The anomaly had apparently been shadowing a large school of fish. The school of fish; according to the data the virtual system was displaying, had been numbering less and less every twenty minutes or so. The data indicated smaller objects exited and returned to the larger one. The smaller objects were almost identical in structure and form.

Using data from the UKNI-Net web the APLR's found a match. The objects weren't machines of any known design. Their structure resembled creatures UKNI-Net matched to life forms that were recently reported to have attacked a newly quarantined town in the state of Tennessee.

In the HUD of Commander Edwards helmet, he watched the recording as Dr. Muerte explained,

Video Recording: Dr. Phrezel Muerte:

"The biological breakdown of the creature's genetic structure was somewhat curious. It doesn't have a simple two-sided DNA sequence like humans and the majority of life indigenous to Earth. Instead, it has a third strand of nucleic acids. This third strand isn't composed of the usual nucleic acids within the human genome. It appears to be composed of a complex order of iron, sulfur & silicate-based acids. Upon test injections into different cell types, the genetic material causes some strange reactions."

The screen changed to display a split screen with a diagram of the genetic structure along with a microscope view as Muerte continued, "This third chain replicates itself by actually rearranging the DNA patterns of the host animal cell to mirror its own. Then it began reorganizing the functions of the cell, producing large amounts of complex hydrocarbons. When it was injected into the nucleus of a plant cell, it changed the structure so drastically that the cell wall was simply consumed from within. The only plant cell structures that were not essentially obliterated were the ribosome and mitochondria. It appears that this creature's basic cellular functions were similar to our own, just composed of a fantastic cocktail of more volatile chemicals."

Returning to the screen excitedly, Muerte animatedly explained, "One of the most significant distinctions is the density of the creature. With the added weight, on a cellular level, of a third strand of nucleic acids composed of these dense molecules, the strength of the creatures had to be formidable. This density also indicates that they had to have evolved in a system relatively close to a white-hot star. Now, locating a galaxy within the calculated region of space, and speculation provided from Commander Edwards wasn't easy. Their galaxy was one that seems to have all but disappeared from that region of astronomically mapped space twenty or so years ago. All that appears to be left of what had been that galaxy is what we now call dark matter. One can only assume that something cataclysmic caused all the stars within that galaxy to go supernova and then cool at a rapid rate. There are numerous astronomical surveys of this region of space which have been recorded in the past few months that indicate something is happening in that galaxy.

The problem is that we have no way of seeing the details due to its distance and the absorbent nature of dark matter."

***

The details the squad received were somewhat sketchy. The downlink from UKNI-net showed highly focused imaging of what had occurred in a small swampy Tennessee town. It also had a few detailed stills from a video camera of an encounter aboard a fishing schooner in which one of the creatures was destroyed a few miles off the Florida coastline.

The information included a log of biological information recovered from Dr. Muerte's examination on the remains of the creature, which had once been young deputy Lomax, in quarantine.

Notably, each of the creatures was of the same species, with differences due only to the incomplete mutation of the young deputy. Once that connection had been established, the only decision left to make was how the Squad would proceed.

Commander Edwards pondered, "Should we go to the island first, or find that vessel that attacked the town and the fishing ship?"
After thinking for a moment, he decided and informed the Squad, "We will go after the vessel first."

He queried UKNI-Net for the island location as a second mission location point, along with any additional details as they became available.
UKNI-Net's response indicated that there was no additional information available.

Whatever was shielding the island was beyond the conventional military equipment and even had UKNI-net guessing at ways to break through. The Squad, scoured through all the data anomalies until one member noted a ship, that was anchored in an unusual place.

Closer scanning revealed it to be a private vessel registered as *The Aquaticus*. Another anomaly was located traveling along their same trajectory a few miles ahead of them, toward the island. This vessel matched the one indicated in one of the recent quarantine reports and resembled the one in their mission briefing.

The Squad increased their speed and ascension toward the surface so they would reach the island before the threatening vessel. They could then set up an excellent defensive position until they were required to intervene.

As they came within ten miles of the island, they left the water and took to the skies. The monitoring members of the APLR's noted a drastic shift in the ocean floor beneath the island. Their data, transmitted by UKNI-net, was incomplete due to the island's shielding which made it impossible to get a visual.

Approaching the target zone, they encountered tremendous amounts of turbulence that would have crushed a normal airplane like tin foil. Thanks to the intervention of the Nygic technology and some truly talented scientists who were able to convert theory into reality; they punched through the turbulence with minor course adjustments and a small amount of fancy piloting.

Once they breached the inner sphere of the island's turbulent shielding, they were dazed by what they saw. They hadn't just punched through condensed windstorms, but also a dome of water.

It seemed, upon quick examination of incoming data fields, that the water level within the shielded area had begun to increase disproportionately to the levels outside of the protected zone. The entire region around the island was becoming a freestanding hydro dome. The idea in itself was inconceivable by traditional physics, but so was the manipulation of DNA on the level which the Squad had experienced. They accepted this strange phenomenon and adjusted their ships configuration accordingly.

The ship's black luster became shiny as the wings withdrew and it descended gently toward the water. They submerged and descended until they were parallel with the position of the island. As they traveled toward the central region, the APLR's Advanced Artificial Intelligence (A2I) systems indicated that the two surface zones were aquatically inert. The water hadn't been simply rising but had also enclosed them within a protective bubble or terrestrially supportive bubble.

Once they reached the island, their TA-3's reconfigured for an aquatic atmosphere. This allowed an easily adjustable flow of water to pass through so that the Squad members could breathe the oxygen from the surrounding water.

Four scouts took up directional positions along the outer isle's aquatic perimeter while four secondary scouts took the back up positions within the land zone of the perimeter isle.

The vehicles morphed and split into four separate vehicles, one for each Squad member. This was something that had not been included in the briefing about the vehicular features. The Squad members were slightly surprised.

One Squad member verbalized, "Well, that's just awesome, did anyone know that the APLR's could do that?"

Commander Edwards responded, "You may find that there are many things not included in our briefings that we might discover on the fly."

There were three smaller, sleeker ships which could morph freely and one bulky ship that contained the Squads equivalent of heavy artillery. The other four teams headed toward the inner isle. It was a fantastic sight. It was a free-standing aquatic structure, with no solid supports of any kind.

Edwards lead his team on a quick, oblique perimeter path around the island before heading for the lower cavernous region. As they descended to the cavernous region underneath land level, the APLR sensors noted that the ship was being bombarded with electric currents. Though the voltage was so minimal that it caused no damage, Edwards asked the system to identify the cause and noted what appeared to be giant Moray eels. Noting that they weren't any threat to the Quantum Flux armor, he ordered his team to avoid the eels.

A long-distance radial scan was performed for the locations of more eel groupings. They noted that the eels were located in a loose but even grid and that the ones that attacked, apparently noticing that they had no effect directly went back to their respective conditions. Edwards and the remaining seven Squad members headed toward the cave-like entrance under the rim of the inner isle.

While maneuvering toward the rim, they were almost sideswiped by a pair of aggressive serpentine creatures. They zigged and zagged along sporadically and lunged themselves at the APLR's. At first, the Squad members avoided these creatures as well also, but it became more of a hassle to keep evading their attacks.

Intending to ram the creatures as their paths intersected, knowing that the Quantum armor would protect them, they increased their speed. When the APLR warned of imminent structural damage, which would occur if such tactics were employed, the Squad was taken aback. At Commander Edwards ordered, "return to evasive maneuvers," the Squad members punched the turbine engines once they reached a safe distance from the creatures. The creatures pursued, but only briefly. The gap between them widened, and the creatures abruptly changed their directions until they were finally out of sight.

Wondering what could have gone wrong, the Squad put the APLR's into shadow mode. Shadow mode allowed the engines to perform off a revolutionary super conductive electro-magnetically self-contained turbine engine. As they were supercooled, the engines, as well as their crafts, were invisible to anything using heat signatures as a guide to their location.

Chapter 32

Within the confines of the Trigener' vessel, Ronaw saw that four objects were approaching the island. These objects were at first present in the marine environment, then they seemed to ascend from the water and fly. At first, he thought, "these are some additional genetically altered living weapons of the Trigener." But they were moving too rapidly. They appeared as a series of white voids on the screen. So Ronaw turned to Lakur and asked, "What are those white voids?"

Lakur studied the display again and rubbed his hand along the fuzzy controller causing another set of strange symbols to appear next to the objects.

Taken aback Lakur said, "It appears to be some type of ship."

Lakur moved his hands along the bio-vessels console with such gentleness it seemed as if he was comforting a small child. The area increased in viewing size. The four items changed shape as they went from the marine environment to air. They also changed in proportion as they divided into a total of sixteen separate vehicles. Four vehicles took up what looked like directional positions at four equidistant points around the perimeter of the outer island. Once in place, they maintained position with an occasional movement to avoid collision with the other aquatic residents.

Lakur pointed out "These ships are not entirely of earth's origin." He made a few more motions on the console, and the display magnified the ships, placing a strange grid over them. Upon seeing this Lakur let out a gasp, along with the rest of the passengers.

"I'm not 100 percent certain, but I recognize the shielding matrix of the vehicles," Lakur said absently.

"Look at the way they are shrugging off the eel's attacks, with no effect. Let's see what happens when the Velithians strike?" Lakur said, focused on the display.

While watching the vehicles interact with the defensive creatures, it was noted that the vehicles seemed to disappear from the screen for brief moments. For a moment it was as if the vehicles were destroyed, perhaps by the damage that was sustained from the various life forms it was encountering, then Lakur said, "No! The vehicles are using camouflage."

Seeing that the security team and Ronaw were confused by his statement, he began to explain.

"In the galaxy that human astronomers labeled as Nygic 101, there was a race of beings that can control the emanation of heat from their bodies as well as their vessels, making them all but invisible to any creatures that use heat for guidance to its target. They can also control a substantial amount of light reflection, refraction and absorption. We called them the Illusri, which loosely translates in the English language to the word "phantoms." We attempted to contact them by traveling to the last known locations of a few of their worlds, but we could never find them. Our scientists believed that the myths about them were just that, myths."

Ronaw replied, "So let me get this right, with your advanced scientific technology, you missed an entire planet? How could the Trigener miss an entire planet?"

Lakur stopped looking at the screen for a moment, and it seemed as if his mind was thousands of miles away.

Deep in thought, it was a while before Lakur finally replied.

"At first our scientist believed that their calculations were incorrect, that they had overshot the Illusri home-worlds positions by several solar rotations. Then they realized that they had not missed anything, the planets were nearby, our scientist just had no way to see them. This race of phantoms were masters of this technology. They had to be to make entire planets, even entire inhabited solar systems visibly and gravitationally disappear."

"What did your people do, since they could not find this Illusri civilization?" Ronaw inquired.

"We left a beacon in the hope that this race of beings would retrieve the beacon and decipher the data about our dilemma as we worked to survive the Charcomanti attacks. Maybe they would be able to help us in some way," explained Lakur.

Gina chimed in, "As far as we know, there are no other survivors from our world. Only those present in this chamber and within this vessel, some of which you saw as we moved through the tunnels to get to this chamber."

Lakur added, "It seems that the Illusri did get our message, and contacted someone on Earth, resulting in the vessels we have just observed."

***

Commander Edwards linked up with the other Squad members via the mini-hyper terminal display within his uniforms HUD. Upon verifying that everyone had taken up their designated co-ordinates around the island, he took four of the squad members with him as he proceeded to the opening of the cave. They moved through the tunnels with the swiftness of piranha. He guided his APLR along and thought, "This is too easy."

Easy made him anxious, allowing his overactive imagination to daunt him with strange thoughts. He shook off the dark urges of his mind and forced his focus on the caverns they were traversing. As they reached the inner portion of the tunnel, he cautiously guided his team through the illuminated gelatinous regions of one of the innermost caves.

They recorded the path that they took to reach the inner underwater caverns. The highly advanced micro-atomic computers on board constantly scanned the surrounding cavern walls and displayed the findings. Edwards was elated to see that the walls were actually composed of some type of biological tissue. They entered a vertical column which, from what they could tell, ended in a softly glowing lighted orifice.

***

UKNI-net's ever-watching eyes were passively keeping track of the Charcomanti vessel. Now, having a name to associate with this un-Earthly vessel, and a small but fundamental understanding of the nature of the violent creatures within, UKNI-net used all resources to find something else which could be used to fight them.

Given the fact that UKNI-Net was a continuously growing and evolving bio-computer, it had at its disposal multiple space-based manufacturing stations and tools. It took control of several robots and began designing an undisclosed weapon. The high ranking, scientific, military minds that saw to the biological and mechanical well-being of UKNI-nets superstructures noticed a small change in the calculations that were taking place in the constant data-spreads downloaded once an hour to a massive seven-mile-long and eighteen hundred feet deep sub-terrain 200x speed high-density digital disk recording storage facility.

UKNI-net, having a human mind, along with a computer's ability, used both thought and calculation at blistering speeds. It realized that it would take years for the human military minds to comprehend what it was doing and why. It didn't attempt to hide its activities, nor did it do anything to bring unnecessary attention to them either. It didn't have time waste.

UKNI ordered two orbiting ice processing collectors to dump their payload into two self-sealing orbital water distillation tanks. The tanks, being convex at the bottom and top, when the transparent shelters were in place, would melt the ice and filter out any impurities making the water inside pure for consumption. Once the water was pure UKNI-Net began the process of freezing the water evenly over the next two hours. This would produce two sheets of ice with a shallow depth of four feet around the perimeter and gradually increase to the deepest depth of seven feet. The end result would be a naturally pure set of magnifying lenses with a radius of thirty meters.

During the freezing process, it also took control of a set of Black Code Military Stealth Satellites. Positioning them close to UKNI-nets central command node, the maintenance robots were used to reprogram the propulsion commands so that the satellites wouldn't be able to return to their predetermined orbits. UKNI-net connected a set of circuit probes to the BCMSS's and began decoding their security systems.

The programming was quite simple actually, it only took UKNI about ten minutes to disarm the tampering system, re-sequence the initiator for the nuclear generators and reprogram the circuitry for a new purpose. One advantage of having the mind of a human joined with the speed of a computer was that it could always remain many steps ahead of either on its own.

***

Commander Edwards proceeded to ascend inside the hollow column that stretched from the end of the tunnel upwards toward something unbeknownst to him. The mini-APLR unit morphed itself into a vertical standing, torpedo-shaped vessel. This also forced Edwards body into an upright position, as the internal control interfaces now fit snugly against his body. He moved slowly upward, scanning every inch of the way for possible danger.

The water within the tunnel steadily increased in warmth until it reached a comfortable sixty-eight degrees. Using the Mini-APLR'S versatility, he allowed for the water to filter through unhindered after a quick sample indicated no contaminants were present. It only took seven minutes to reach the termination of the tubule. It emptied out into a vast cave-like orifice that scans indicated was composed of the same bio-material as the caverns below.

The scans also indicated that the cavern had more than one room and was occupied by various beings of humanoid appearance. A few of the occupant's outward physical appearance was human, but their inner physical structure was somewhat unstable, almost in a constant state of flux. As the APLR's emerged from the water, many of the occupants gathered within a sort of passageway which sealed itself off rapidly from the cavern that the APLR's were now occupying.

Chapter 33

The Charcomanti hive seethed with contempt for the soft fleshed creatures of this world. Once they dealt with the remnants of the Trigener' that resided on this island within this Earth, they would signal for an all-out assault to eradicate all life on this planet.

As they drew closer to the isle, the movement in the hive became more restless at the thought of the potential slaughter of the Trigener'. Those gelatinous creatures were no match for the sleek, powerfully evolved Charcomanti. Swarm attack was the method they used, quick, deadly, and crushing.

The world the Trigener came from was so pathetic. No weapons and no will to fight, it was so easy to destroy them. Their race needed to be destroyed. They were weak, a blight on the universe. They did resist, but they were swiftly overpowered by the rightful warlords of the Charcomanti race. Now, these warlords had found the Trigener's last remnants, on a new planet to conquer and claim.

The Charcomanti would look back upon this day and thank the memory of the Trigener' species for this new planet. They would go back to the gaseous planet in this solar system, inform their kindred of this world, and return home to their galaxy. Then, they would return with enough reinforcements to bring another world under the hive's realm of rule.

***

Upon completion of the scans, which indicated no overt hostile life forms present, Commander Edwards ordered his squad to dismount from their vehicles and attempt contact with the inhabitants of the vessel. The APLR's were linked with the TA3 uniforms so that in an emergency they would locate their counterparts and provide rapid retrieval, defense, or escape if necessary.

The vehicles hovered stealthily in place just above the water. They disturbed nothing, made no noise aside from a soft low rumble within the confines of the caverns. They looked like huge gemstones. They were a silver-ish, translucent material. They rippled with life, as they were an extension, separate parts of a whole being.

Edwards and a few selected squad members dismounted from their vehicles. The rest of the squad stayed behind, watching in silence as their team phased through the surface skin of their vessels. There was only a brief opening through which the members slipped out, as the opening sealed itself immediately leaving no sign of a disturbance.

The team dropped quietly into the pools below. As the team tread water in the pool, they made their way to the solid surface just as the walls of the vessel's interior began to shift and gelatinous material oozed down to form a transparent partition between the squad and its passengers. The wall looked very flimsy, like thin saran wrap. As the Squad attempted to walk through it, they were rejected by an unseen force.

Having detected no discernible power source, the APLR's simply hovered where they were. Confused by what they had experienced, the Squad members looked at each other. After a few moments of deliberation, and some sort of communication between the members of the Squad, some nodding and pointing, Edwards decided to remove his helmet.

Upon his example, the other two Squad members removed theirs as well. The cavern was quiet. Commander Edwards and his Squad mates tried to scan the minds of the people they were viewing through the wall.

Dr. Ronaw was charged. Not only had he seen most of the people who came with him, transformed into things he had no real words to describe, but now he felt as though he was having a flashback from his childhood. The creatures before him now had enlarged craniums, elongated eyes, and rather small mouths and tiny remnants of nasal protrusions. These people were humanoid. They looked somewhat like the descriptions given by people, who claimed that they had been abducted, would describe.

He thought to himself, *I would not believe this story if I wasn't here, right now, to see it.*

Commander Edwards tuned into Ronaw's mind as he thought, *If I hadn't been present to see the sights of the last two days, I would still be a skeptic.*

After a few moments of pregnant silence, the bio-vessels interior partition dissipated, leaving nothing between the Squad and the passengers which had already been aboard. The gold uniformed Squad member walked towards them slowly, trying not to appear aggressive.

Lakur stepped to the head of the group in front of the golden humanoid and extended his hand. The golden clad humanoid grabbed Lakur's hand, and as their hands touched, the coating from the gold creatures arm slithered out and wrapped itself around their hands leaving them joined at the wrist.

As Lakur stood, hand in hand with the humanoid, their eyes locked in an intense gaze. Each of the men moved and jerked lightly several times. It seemed like they were involved in a test of strength, but it was more than that. Lakur and the golden humanoid were engaged in an in-depth mental exchange. They exchanged a lot of information in those few moments, mind to mind, which would have taken them days or even weeks to exchange verbally.

***

The Charcomanti reached the perimeter of the hydrosphere which encompassed billions of metric tons of water, held in place by some unknown force. They were somewhat hindered by their curiosity, from their current objective. They had not seen such a sight before.

Their vessel circled the hydrosphere several times before it attempted to enter the sphere. To their consternation, the outer skin of the sphere became hard and solid. The vehicle bumped up against the shell of the sphere several times before emitting a sonic frequency that caused the immediate area in front of the Charcomanti vessel to return to its liquified form. The Charcomanti vessel charged into the sphere of water.

A few moments after being submerged in the water the belly of the craft parted and the creatures within it spilled forth. The writhing mass of bodies dispersed slowly, seeking out anything that moved under its own power.

The first things it encountered were a group of abnormally large Moray eels. The first Charcomanti to confront the eels were shocked, literally. One Charcomanti had grabbed an eel with the intention of crushing the life out of it, but the electricity generated by the creature was disproportionate to its size. The Charcomanti claw and arm exploded in a quick release from the pulse of energy. Though the original Moray eel was now free, the Charcomanti was still rendered paralyzed as more of the Morays attacked and shocked the beast until it was rigid and no longer a threat.

A few more of the Charcomanti were taken out by the surprise attack from the first wave of Moray eels, but, the Charcomanti swarm was quick to recover. They adjusted and swam defensively to avoid more of the attacking eels. They swam in a tight formation, dispersing randomly only to avoid the incoming eel attacks. The eels regrouped and attacked in a disbursing star pattern. They dove towards the heart of the swarm and then spread out, dispatching a few more of the Charcomanti swarm.

The squad's members quietly watched as the battle progressed. Their orders were to observe until Commander Edwards indicated that they were needed.

***

Inside the Steorscip, Lakur and Commander Edwards released their handshake just as the floor began vibrating. The display focused in on a section of the hydrosphere. It showed a diamond-shaped vessel extruding numerous creatures, identified as a threat. The creatures were immediately assaulted by the mutated moray eels. Out of the initial wave of Charcomanti, only about seven or eight were eliminated or injured. Two or three more of the attacking creatures were taken out by a few more of the electric eels, but the remaining creatures recovered and performed extremely tight, evasive maneuvers.

The entire group, numbering about 45 moved in the water like one massive beast. As the eels attempted to penetrate the heart of the mass, the number of eels slowly began to dwindle. More reinforcements sprang from different areas along the island's perimeter, but to no avail. The group of Charcomanti began to perform hit and runs to draw the eels apart, and then they struck quickly.

The eels, with all their intelligence, were simply outmaneuvered as their numbers dwindled and reinforcements were almost exhausted. The remaining eels retreated to the caverns and caves of the underwater structures of the island.

The Charcomanti regrouped casually. Some of them straggled around a few fallen comrades. They seemed to be checking for survivors, maybe they were mourning the fallen. Once they finished surveying their fallen, the Charcomanti again began their journey run towards the opening which led into the inner chambers of the bio-vessel. Upon recognizing the intentions of the Charcomanti, Lakur ran his hand along the console activating their secondary defenses.

The Charcomanti were headed toward the entrance cave. Their claws were extended in anticipation. The Velitheans, which were still a good distance ahead of where the Charcomanti were going, sliced through the water increasing their speed. They paralleled one another and curved their angle so that they would intersect amidst the Charcomanti. The speed at which they glided back and forth through the water was blinding.

The Charcomanti began to slowly disburse their group, providing more space between one another. The Velitheans plunged through the horde and struck several of the Charcomanti creatures with their diamond-sharp scales. A few Charcomanti were ripped in half while other unfortunate Charcomanti were scraped by the scales of the first attack and lost a few appendages.

The injured Charcomanti made a hasty retreat to the vessel from which they had come. As the Velitheans chased the widespread Charcomanti all over the sphere, occasionally causing severe injury, the Charcomanti lost their immediate interest in the entrance to the caverns.

One of the Velitheans pursued a Charcomanti, shadowing its banking motions until the razor-sharp scales on its face pierced through the back of the creature. The Velithean continued to pick up speed as its head exited the frontal thorax of the Charcomanti and a billowing yellowish cloud of Charcomanti blood expanded from the gaping hole. Its body became utterly transparent as the Velithean turned sharply back toward the slowly descending body and plowed through its remains.

Chapter 34

UKNI-Net continued moving its components as fast as it could without destroying any irreplaceable pieces by mistake. It maneuvered several large solar reflectors into a huge oblique X matrix, at the center of which was a substantial concave gold-plated mirror. These very components had been used over the past six decades to reflect the heat from the sun over the western and eastern coastal regions to softly thaw out fruit groves which had suffered unexpectedly from untimely climate change. This would be the greatest engineering feat by any one being, even though the intelligence involved was far beyond any ever known before on Earth.

The moisture collectors ejected two huge lens-shaped slabs of ice. UKNI knew that even though the lenses were in space, they could still only be used consecutively about four times. The heat from the solar reflectors would be intensified at least ten times due to their overlapping. Thus, even though in space water freezes almost instantaneously, the lenses would less effective with each use. This calculation indicated that the current lenses would only be viable for 3 to 5 uses.

The good thing about the reflectors was that

they all had a set of hyper-pivots and hyper-responsive navigational thrusters on them. The thrusters allowed the navigational units to retrieve its programming from UKNI-net and deploy on their own. They would only fire engines to keep within their programmed orbits and distance parameters, so when they were called upon to act, they would respond for the appropriate amount of time indicated then turn their reflectors away from the main concave reflector. Performing in this fashion, they wouldn't have a constant flow of the sun's energy melting the lenses.

The lenses were positioned by an independent set of eight range response drones. These drones stayed tightly within their programmed parameters and very rarely lost position without some form of direct intervention. Four drones held each lens in predetermined orbits awaiting instructions from UKNI-net.

It planned to use the mirrors to reflect a set of highly focused beams of solar energy at the Charcomanti vessel. The heat, although only equal to 1 thousandth of the sun's direct energy reading, would, though diminished by the Earth's atmosphere, ignite any substance with its beam due to the beams critically high flashpoint. Based on the calculations that UKNI-net made, that should be more than enough to destroy any member of the Charcomanti and do serious damage to the vessel in which they traveled.

***

The APLR'S vibrated in sync with the pool of water inside the vessel. Their reflective silver coatings shimmered like small pools of mercury. Lakur dashed over to the console and grazed his hand across imperceptible grooves. The battle ensuing outside was fierce.

Somehow, the Charcomanti had tricked the Velitheans into ramming one another head first. They did no real damage to each other, but they did show considerable sluggishness and lower maneuverability than before. Maybe the impact dazed them because they began to retreat to their hidden lairs beneath the outer island ring. While trying to retreat, one of the Velitheans was attacked by some Charcomanti, barraged from every direction.

Lakur zoomed in on the action and could see, only by the color variations that the Velithean was in danger. Several of its massive scales, all located around the region just behind the creature's head were picked off, giving the Charcomanti easy access to its soft flesh.

The Velithean would have died had its partner not counter-attacked with a swift looping dive, beheading the unaware Charcomanti. They disbursed immediately and backed away from the retreating Velitheans.

***

Edwards slid his helmet on, and it immediately contorted and shifted until it conformed to his uniform and resealed. He nodded in Lakur's direction, and Lakur nodded back. The other team members donned their helmets followed Edwards back toward their vehicles.

The APLR'S ascended toward the thinnest region at the top of the cavern. Below them, the tunnel had all but sealed itself completely.

Within the tunnel, Lakur shouted, "Dr. Ronaw and the security team members who are not Trigener, please enter the compartments containing the gel before you. These are escape pods, inside which you would be safely transported to the surface of the Steorscip."

As Dr. Ronaw entered the pod nearest him, the material molded itself to the shape of his body and a console protruded upward from the cushion he sat on. It wasn't a standard console; it was sort of like a directional controller with a propulsion indicator. He looked through the side of his pod and saw that Lakur and the other Trigener' began to return to their alien forms. It was beautiful, the innards of the cavern glowed with their gradually increasing, wondrous dance of light.

The region of the pod directly in front of Dr. Ronaw began to display some diagram. At the same time, a gelatinous helmet restraint engulfed his head firmly. He was initially alarmed but as he calmed himself, all the images he had been observing, were now being painted softly into his mind. He began to understand what he was seeing.

It was straightforward; they were quick instructional images indicating how he'd control the vessel should he need to escape.

As Edwards and the Squad members propelled through the opening at the top of the cavern, they went from an extremely moist atmosphere to an ear-popping, humid, enclosed atmosphere.

They were within a bubble within the hydrosphere above the inner island. The land mass beneath them was completely dry. Myriads of indescribable life forms moved and shifted positions as they watched the battle around them within the water of the hydrosphere. They had no idea of the danger. Many of the creatures inhabiting the surface of both Isles had never encountered humans nor the Charcomanti, so they watched the moving shadows with interest. They watched the shadows move to and fro in a never changing all-encompassing deep blue sky.

***

Within the Steorscip, Lakur was working feverishly along with a few of the survivors to coordinate their defenses with the actions of the Squad. They recalled the eels so that they wouldn't attack the Squad member's vessels. The Velithean's were safely re-cocooned inside the perimeter isles stasis cavities, undergoing biomedical reconstruction to repair the damage inflicted by the Charcomanti attack.

Chapter 35

The APLR's breached the inner bubble and penetrated into the waters waiting behind an unseen gate. There was no change within the inner bubble, its many inhabitants simply continued with their daily existence with an occasional glance towards the dancing shadows in the water.

Edwards gave the signal for his squad to enter the battle. According to the HUD, about twenty-eight of the Charcomanti were still trying to reach the inner isle. The injured had all but retreated back to the safety of their hive-vessel.

The APLR'S intelligence and responses were extremely swift, the units immediately formed a defensive line. Each APLR fused with the uniform of the nearest Squad member, or the member riding within. Some of the Squad converted their APLR to an exoskeleton configuration. Within their now humanoid shaped APLR'S the Squad selected their special, mission acquired, explosive tipped rocket artillery. Locked and loaded, they selected their targets and closed in.

The Squad struck at the Charcomanti with prejudice. An unsuspecting Charcomanti was beheaded by a swift cross-chopping arm motion of one of the Squad-members. A few of the Squad remained in their amphibious vehicle modes. They attacked the Charcomanti with a continuous barrage of the super-heated rockets that drilled through the Charcomanti armor and smoldered until they ignited the fluid inside and the creature cooked from the inside out. This left a stiff, semi-rigid shell that collapsed as the pressure of the water pushed the trapped air free.

Edwards was not one who believed in standing idly by as his soldiers fought around him. He headed straight for the mother ship. His APLR spat him forward adding its momentum to his at his mental command. He dove towards the hive as his TA-3 uniform became a suit of super sharp jagged edges. He aimed for the bulbous region of the Charcomanti vessel. The vessels outer hull opened up as he dove toward its surface and he was swallowed inside.

Edwards was disoriented for a moment by this development and the darkness, but not enough to drop his defenses.

Speaking out loud, though to himself, he quietly stated, "Well... that wasn't very smart." He knew that entering the vessel had been too easy. He pondered some of the possible reasons quickly. If he was in their position, letting an enemy combatant breach your defenses would be acceptable for many reasons; mainly because the enemy would be at a disadvantage. This bothered him.

The Charcomanti inside gathered around

him rapidly. Edwards could see their eyes get closer. He thought, "Are they planning to attack me from all angles?"

If that were the plan, he was definitely outmatched. This maneuver would have overwhelmed him just as it would any other enemy. Only, he was inside the ship for a few moments, and nothing had happened.

"What's going on?" He thought.

All of a sudden, his TA-3 uniform spasmed gently within the gel-like substance that surrounded him. It was like a strong sneeze that sent tingles through his entire body. At first, he thought it was a quirk in the uniform, or perhaps his random thoughts were causing a confused reaction from his armor, but it happened again, and more violently as he tried to focus on his current objective. He gradually realized that the armor was getting relatively warmer. He held his hand up before his face and looked closer at it.

The acuity of the uniform far surpassed his normal sight, and he could see that the temperature of the suit had increased five degrees higher than the surrounding gel. He didn't understand as he looked around for some reason to explain this occurrence. His Hud focused in on each of the Charcomanti, lulling about him. They were observing him. They weren't attacking, and he still hadn't figured out why. He glanced back at his hand and noticed that it was no longer covered in jagged edges. Was this gel causing his suit a problem? He thought about it and began to slowly inch his way toward the nearest wall. He felt a lot of resistance.

"What's going on? Think man, think!" Edwards said aloud. It was the substance inside the ship, somehow it was interfering with the connection between his mind and the suit. He didn't understand why, but he knew that even with his training and increased speed and strength he wouldn't last long all by himself. He focused his thoughts on the Squad members and projected his predicament toward their minds. He also opened an audio transmission and firmly requested, "Assistance needed!"

As he moved slowly toward the nearest wall of the vessel, one of the Charcomanti, guardedly inched towards him. The illumination within the vessel increased moderately so that he could see clearly around him. About twelve Charcomanti were observing him and one humongous, insectoid creature which appeared to be molded into the wall of the vessel.

Edwards spoke to himself, "That's definitely a cause for concern." It watched him also. It had a head full of eyes, but it was distinctly different from the other Charcomanti. It had a similar cranial structure, but it also had three horns. One horn protruded from the lower region of the creature's facial features just below what he considered a chin. The other two horns curved forward toward the front of the creature on either side of its head. The neck of the beast was segmented like a centipede with several whip-like appendages on either side. Below its neck, the creature's body was massive but appeared soft like a huge slug. He couldn't see beyond that point because its body merged physically with the ship.

It was at least three times the size of the rest of the Charcomanti. Maybe it was the king or queen of the hive.

"That's definitely the leader," Edwards spoke aloud to himself. As he moved closer to the wall, Edwards curled his body up in a tight ball and used every bit of mental energy he could muster to force his armor to create a bubble shield around himself. He tried to delve back through the inner wall of the vessel outward. It reacted by getting thicker.

It was somehow aware like his armor. As it increased its thickness around his shielding, Edwards opened several small portals in his cocoon and released several of the superheated darts into the vessels skin. The vessels reaction to the darts was instantaneous. There was a quick pulling motion and a violent push that propelled Edwards outside of the vessel into the water again.

***

Taxed from the ordeal, Edwards mentally signaled his APLR, which had been waiting not far outside of the vessel. The APLR sprang to life, engulfed him, and immediately signaled that the uniform had been exposed to some chemical compound. The APLR opened several intake and outtake ventilation gills and circulated the water at an extremely high speed around Edwards. A few minutes passed before the chemical levels were low enough that they weren't causing any more interference between Edwards and the uniform. It was then that Edwards realized, none of his team appeared to be responding to his call for help.

Meanwhile, the Charcomanti within the vessel were active again. This time the vessel changed shape and slowly extended its length while decreasing its width. It looked like a long jet-black rod. Then the color changed to a forest green color, with patches of dark teal at six evenly spaced intervals along its length.

The squad members had all but annihilated the Charcomanti that were outside of the vessel during the Commander Edwards absence. As he accounted for his team, he noted that they were rounding up the last Charcomanti and were corralling them toward the eel caves.

Seeing that the caves were dark, the Charcomanti dove into them. They expected the assailants to follow them into the darkness. They were misled. Once they were within the cave, a huge bed of seaweed like material gently closed off the entrance blocking all light. This did not bother the Charcomanti, darkness was an ally. One of the Charcomanti felt something slide, lightly along one of its legs. It reached out but felt nothing.

Then there it was again, something pressing gently against its leg. And then there was another something resting against another leg. Each of the caved Charcomanti experienced the random touching of something smooth at random spots along their carapaces. Within seconds, the Moray eels engulfed them synchronizing their electric charge concurrently, instantaneously frying the Charcomanti group into hard, solid statues; which smoldered and popped open to spill out their innards.

As the Charcomanti vessel continued to display seemingly random patterns, the Squad members regrouped. One portion of the team began orbiting the vessel to monitor its actions. Edwards piloted his APLR to the head of the Squads reserve group facing the vessel.

Edwards was monitoring the readouts from the vessel when his helmet flashed an alert. There was an incoming message from UKNI-net. Edwards moved his APLR to the rear of the Squads formation to decipher the incoming data. There were a number of quick flashes of diagrams and schematics, which would simply be a flash of light to a rational human mind, but his transformed mind could digest information at an accelerated speed. Edwards understood the burst of information which he then transmitted to his team, "Squad members, please retreat beyond the parameters I am transmitting."

While the team members were changing their positions, they all observed the continuing changes of the Charcomanti vessel.

***

Meanwhile, in orbit above the island, UKNI-net, using the relative positions of the squad members, and optical transmissions from their helmets, to obtain more precise coordinates on the Charcomanti vessel, performed a series of brief additional calculations to narrow down the area of collateral damage. Upon completion of those calculations, UKNI-Net transmitted coordinates, and the hyper pivots made alterations in their flight path.

UKNI-Net started the countdown to send a highly focused stream of solar light through the ice lenses in an attempt to damage, and ultimately destroy the Charcomanti vessel. UKNI-Net was not 100 percent certain that everything would work as designed, but the theory was sound. UKNI-Net accounted for energy fluctuations around the island and used multiple variables to compensate.

Chapter 36

T-15:00 and counting

While the rest of the squad members fell back, Edwards' APLR, continued the filtering process, which was almost complete. He could tell that his bio-armors response time was returning to normal. A Charcomanti Solidus emerged from the hive's vessel on an intercept course with APLR.

The APLR flashed an alert that Edwards responded to quickly. He used several pivoting thrusters to flip his vehicle over on its axis while allowing his momentum to keep him floating a safe distance. Upside down, but facing the incoming Charcomanti, readouts indicated a slight change in its form.

The outer exoskeleton was twice as thick as the Charcomanti he'd previously faced. Scanning the creature for a weakness, Edwards noticed that the defensive design of this Charcomanti was only beneficial from a head-on attacker position. He released a volley of super-heated darts, which the Charcomanti shielded himself from with one of its plated arms. The darts drilled deep into the armor but did not pierce through and ignite the blood of the beast, and it continued forth with almost no hesitation.

Recognizing the Charcomanti adaptation, Edwards sent a signal for reinforcements to draw its attention away from him. Two additional Squad members responded and joined the conflict. Edwards and his APLR morphed to humanoid battle form. Edwards altered his heading which took him in a circular loop that would if the attacker did not change course, position him directly behind the creature. The Charcomanti began altering its heading when it saw his motion but returned to its original trajectory when the other two APLRS came into view.

***

T-12:50 and counting

As they battled in an effortless engagement with the new Charcomanti, several of the squad members picked up severe tremors emanating from the bio-vessel. They saw many more Charcomanti Solidus, as if propelled by a cannon, enter the tunnel Edwards and the other Squad members had entered before. Unfortunately, they were occupied and had to leave the Bio-vessel and its occupants to fend for themselves for the moment. The water vibrated around them violently several more times.

Halfway along the tunnel route, one segment of the tunnel perimeter began to constrict rapidly just ahead of where the Charcomanti Solidus entered. Then another section began to constrict also just aft of their entry point.

The section of the tunnel ahead of the constriction points collapsed, adhering to the bottom of the vessel and left no entrance where there had once been one. The tunnel region that was severed fell free from the vessel. It sunk downward, toward the ocean floor at the bottom of the hydrosphere. Upon a quick scan one Squad member transmitted that the Charcomanti intruders were encased inside the tunnel segment, and immobilized. The tunnel segment was tagged by a Squad member, with a **TRACE SCAN MONITOR BEACON** that would transmit continuous data on the location of the tunnel fragment and its inhabitants.

***

T-10:00

Making a minor alteration in the revolution speed of the Darts propulsion unit, the two-member Squad team released several of them toward the aggressing Charcomanti Solidus.

The first succession was deflected with several swipes of the Charcomanti armored arm.

The second barrage impacted within close proximity of one another. Being so close they damaged one of the plated arms and reached the Charcomanti blood that ignited, leaving a yellowish trail as the monster flailed its injured arm about in apparent pain.

As Edwards completed his arc and was behind the beast, it took one of its remaining three arms and yanked the injured appendage off.

The self-inflicted wound congealed slowly as the Charcomanti continued its charge at the incoming APLRS. Edwards took aim at the back of the creature's head and fired three darts. When they pierced the Charcomanti's head, the creature immediately convulsed and began flailing its arms about as it turned to face him. The other attacking squad members took aim and released several more volleys at the creature's rear area which sent it descending uncontrollably.

The smoldering carcass bubbled and shook as pockets of air built up inside. The body then imploded as the gases escaped swiftly into the surrounding water. All that was left was the Charcomanti shell that was singed from the inside out. A school of barracuda swimming by savagely attacked the innards of the shell.

***

T-05:30 and counting

The other squad members continued waiting outside the established perimeter set by UKNI-Net. Everyone was antsy, waiting for the opportunity to crush more of the Charcomanti, as Edwards and the others returned to the safety zone.

UKNI-net transmitted some more information to the Squad.

"Squad, regroup and reunite," Edwards ordered after receiving the transmission. The APLRS recombined to reestablish the four original vehicles of the same shape hanging in the water a safe distance from the Charcomanti vessel.

***

The Steorscip, now hovering just above the absolute center of the sphere, began to spin on its axis slowly. The atmospheric bubble on top of it began to expand. The outer Isle began to rise. The ring ascended until its surface was above the sphere of water and no longer needed the atmospheric bubble.

Then the bio-vessel's rotation gradually slowed, and under its own power, it glided upward until its surface was now level with the dry land mass of the outer Isle.

They both hung in the air like hummingbirds causing a small vibration throughout the sphere. The upper surface of the bio-vessel's skin began to slide itself around. The perimeter Isle softly pivoted until its inner face was in direct contact with the surface of the bio-vessel.

The surface of the bio-vessel slithered off and joined itself to the outer island which, upon separating from the bio-vessel, altered its shape into that of an arrow. The bottom of the isle changed color to a burnt orange color and propelled itself free from the aqua-sphere's influence. Once free it simply orbited the sphere.

The Steorscip reclaimed its place at the absolute center of the sphere of water.

***

The Charcomanti vessel had extended several thin curving appendages which joined underneath like a skeletal rib cage. At the aft area of the hive vessel, the tail of the ship bent down and curved rather gracefully like a shrimp tail back towards the front of the vessel. On the tip of the curved tail was a tubule with an orifice inside it. A few armor plated Charcomanti were perched around the rib-like curvatures.

***

T-2:30 and counting

UKNI-net and the Squad were reading an enormous amount of energy building up within the rib-like partitions along the Charcomanti vessel. Edwards and the team ran a series of systems checks to make sure that what they were reading was correct.

The Steorscip began to rotate again on its axis within the sphere of water. It was completely submerged now. There was no atmospheric bubble to maintain, so the vessels surface became smooth and it hung in the water like a perfect shimmering orb. The outer surface began to fold outward at three equidistant points. A ridge formed which ran from the top of the bio-vessel through one of the points down to the bottom. After the ridge grew to about thirty meters in height a second and a third ridge formed with the same dimensions.

The squad members watched what was occurring before their eyes. They monitored the continuous orbit of the arrowhead-shaped Isle floating, safely, and freely, outside of the sphere. They also noticed that the currents within the sphere completely diminished in variety and all turned into one current which ran along the equator of the sphere.

***

T-:60 and counting

Dr. Ronaw and the remaining humans within the bio-vessel noticed that the pods they were in, had begun to move. The light outside of the cocoons abruptly went dark, and they felt motion; slowly at first, like a low pulse rate it moved and stopped repetitively.

As the rate increased, it eventually felt like one continuous motion. They were flung from left to right, then up and down. Dr. Ronaw felt the butterflies of anticipation, excitement and fear. All at once, though the motion stopped, the light outside the cocoons became extremely bright and strong enough to make eyes water. His pod began to darken until it was a dark, reddish-purple, like a ripe pomegranate seed.

This was gentler on the doctor's eyes and

allowed him to see that he was no longer inside the Steorscip. He could see faint wisps of clouds off in the distance. There was the sensation that he was in free-fall.

"Oh no!" Ronaw exclaimed as he realized he was flying through the air in the pod.

He scanned the cocoons memory for a way to be released and whether it would be safe for him to exit. Upon his inquiry, the cocoon indicated where the outer and inner release mechanisms were located. Since the cocoon didn't make him aware of any type of danger, he began to feel about for the mechanisms. Just a few seconds before he placed his hands on them, the cocoon indicated that the oxygen level was lower at this altitude.

"So, I guess I need to wait a bit," Ronaw verbalized.

The doctor waited as he watched the pods external oxygen level indicator. After a few minutes of watching the oxygen gauge creep high enough, he decided he'd take his chances. He was a fit man, he stayed in shape. He recalled his hiking trips in the mountainous regions of Colorado, and deep, prolonged diving trips in the Caribbean.

He thought to himself, "The oxygen level is high enough, I should be able to get out now."

He pressed his hands along the grooves, but the pod would not open. Abruptly, everything went black.

***

The countdown continued. Edwards and his team headed toward the surface of the sphere, hoping to reach safety before the solar beam was fired. Teams 2 and 3 headed for the northernmost point above the bio-vessel. They lined up one on top of the other, tilted the front of their APLR's until the nose was pointed toward the top of the bio-vessel and simply allowed the current to turn them around like spinning tops.

***

First Shot!

Team 4 was attempting to remain in position beyond the Charcomanti ship; however, with the currents being produced by the bio-vessel, they were in a constantly changing orbit. This put them in and out of the line of fire with each revolution. UKNI-net added the new development into its calculations; unfortunately, the acceleration speed of the bio-vessels revolution wasn't consistent. It tried to time the first shot and judge its motion so that the mirrors and lens would move in real-time and remain locked on the Charcomanti vessel. As the mirrors reflected the suns intense rays into a focused stream of light through the ice lenses; the Squad members who were out of the line of fire reflexively held their breath.

The rear half of the Charcomanti vessel was bathed in an intense five-second beam of highly focused solar energy. The APLR, directly aft of the

Charcomanti vessel, was also narrowly struck with that solar stream. Its navigational controls began to falter. The momentum of the current along with gravity propelled it clear of the sphere and down into the ocean. The APLR's outer coating crystallized instantaneously. This kept the APLR from responding to the commands of the Squad members on board. The crystallized shell also locked them inside without a fresh supply of oxygen. The Charcomanti vessel bobbed and shimmied within the beam, and the tail of the vessel exploded as the built-up energy within its tail section erupted. The hive ship oozed a thick black colored gelatinous fluid from its damaged section.

Second Shot!

The second burst of solar energy damaged the rib-like sections of the ship, severing them in half along their equator. The ship leaked more fluid profusely within the lower half of the hydrosphere.

Several of the perched Charcomanti were crisped in place and imploded rapidly upon contact with the burst. The remaining Charcomanti gathered about the large bulbous region of the vessel, trying to protect something on the inside.

Edwards shouted into his helmet, "They are checking for damage to the queen!"

As the squad watched, the bulbous region

constricted at the section closest to the damaged area and the remaining Charcomanti Solidus pulled it free. Seconds after this occurred a high-powered signal of some sort was transmitted from what was left of the Charcomanti vessel.

UKNI-Net tracked the direction of the signal but found that it was wideband, meaning it was almost impossible to predict a specific direction. A few moments after the burst, UKNI-Net transmitted a message to military headquarters about the current status of the island, the Squad and what appeared to be civilians caught in the crossfire. UKNI-Net was slightly confounded by what caused the island to become visible. Maybe it was an energy drain on whatever power source there was keeping the island shielded from scans as it performed actions for defense.

As the Charcomanti Solidus pulled the remains of their vessel toward the surface Edwards and the Squad pursued. The Charcomanti vessel morphed once again while moving, into a flat triangular shape with one triangular tip facing the direction it was going. The two points on either side bent upwards slightly like the wings of stingray. A small thin tail extended from the craft. As it did so, the Charcomanti outside the vessel dissolved into its shell.

"Are these readings correct sir?" One Squad member shouted during the pursuit.

"It appears so, the larger Charcomanti are now inside, and they are decreasing in size,"

Edwards responded. The Charcomanti ship camouflaged itself by making its shell reflective. Commander Edwards and the Squad continued to follow along, recording and marveling at the vessel's activities. Enraptured, they almost forgot about the squad vessel that was slowly sinking down towards the ocean floor.

Edwards alerted the squad members that were still intact and monitoring the island to send a unit down to retrieve their fallen team. The nearest group dove towards the ocean through the pillar of water which seemed to be supporting the hydrosphere. While they were doing so, the scanner tracking the encased Solidus stopped transmitting. Alerted to the new development, the combined APLR split in half and the second unit deployed towards the last known coordinates of the beacon.

The Charcomanti vessel broke the surface of the water and propelled itself towards the sky. Edwards' team of APLR followed suit. Their APLR had morphed into a streamlined flight configuration as they gained on the Charcomanti vessel.

"Where is it going?" Edwards inquired as the Charcomanti ship flew upwards through a dense group of clouds. The ship abruptly banked downward and then up as the rear half of the vessel began to glow an eerie forest green. In response, Edwards launched a miniature transponder missile toward the Charcomanti craft. As it closed the distance, the rear end of the Charcomanti vessel began to change color to florescent green. Within a few feet of impact, a small tube extended from the transponder missile's nose cone. When the missile touched the shell of the vessel, it injected an insect-sized robot.

The robot, propelled at high speed, pierced the shell of the Charcomanti vessel and remained embedded within the crafts inner crust. The Charcomanti vessel angled toward space and in a flash, disappeared from view. Edwards couldn't see the vessel, but he knew, if the robot worked properly, they'd be able to track the vessel.

Adair Rowan

Chapter 37

The rescue APLR team closed in on the damaged one, as it slowly sank below the Hydrosphere. Scans indicated that it was no longer operating under its own power. Those same scans suggested that the water pressure at that depth was what kept their friends from sinking farther.

They transmitted several signals to the APLR and received no reply. As they orbited the inoperable APLR, they used sonar to get a visual image, which indicated a breach in the crystallized shell. Upon examining the hole, it appeared to have been breached from the inside.

Just as they were about to exit their APLR, sensors indicated movement off in the distance. The computer systems immediately locked onto the movement and displayed the findings at high resolution.

They could just make out their Squad mates in a fierce struggle with the Charcomanti Solidus that escaped from the discarded tubule ejected from the Steorscip vessel. The battle was like a quiet dance from a distance. Neither side was gaining or losing ground.

Until the rescue team arrived and shot a massive barrage of the superheated darts. The alerted squadmates mirrored the APLR's movements thereby avoiding the incoming barrage of darts as the Solidus smoldered, blistered and imploded. The rescued Squad group swam up and combined with their rescuer's craft.

***

No longer threatened, the Steorscip's motion decreased rapidly and it slowly descended. The protrusions began to dwindle into nothingness. The currents in the water slowed also and the living island returned to its original appearance. All of the water that made up the standing hydrosphere receded back into the depths of the ocean.

***

Dr. Ronaw opened his eyes to pain, "Oww!"

Nelson from the security team was standing over him with a concerned look on his face.

"Doctor Ronaw, are you o.k.?" he asked urgently.

"Unh, I think so, nothing seems broken," Ronaw replied in angst.

"Wow, I can't believe you're o.k. Doc, that was quite the impact." Nelson explained.

"What impact? What are you talking about?" Ronaw asked earnestly.

"Oh, well you wouldn't remember, but I watched you. You opened your pod before it landed on the island's surface. When you did this, the pod's gravity dampening field was abruptly terminated. I saw you bite the dust, Doc, and I was a little worried." Nelson elucidated.

"So that's why I feel like I've been run over by a truck?" Ronaw inquired.

"Yes sir, but I'm glad that it was the island's surface, because you are still amongst the living." Nelson imparted.

"Me too, Nelson, Me too. Any idea how we can blow this popsicle stand?" Ronaw quizzed.

"Well, it looks like the island, Steorscip, is returning to normal, and hopefully the Lakur ship is still anchored out there." Nelson expressed.

"I hope so," Ronaw retorted.

***

The APLR team lead by Commander Edwards returned from their pursuit of the Charcomanti craft. The remaining APLRS exited the water to greet them as they arrived just outside of the outer island's perimeter.

Standing on the outer island Dr. Ronaw and the security team from Aquaticus observed the final adjustments to the ring. The ground moved and shifted, and the different foliage and life forms slid along without protest. The three sides dipped outward, and the pointed edges fell inward until it was again a complete circle. The water which had engulfed the Steorscip had already been welcomed back into the ocean. The Squad backed away in a tight formation, their equipment recording all that happened around them.

"The brass is going to love this," Edwards said as he thought about the upcoming debriefing.

He wondered to himself, "Who will ever find out what happened today; how the worlds fate rested in the hands of a few men and women, untested science and the gifts of two different race of non-human life forms."

Captain Edwards fired off a beacon that the Naval Reticence teams could use to locate the island. He noticed that the Lakur Yacht hadn't drifted far away from the island during everything that had occurred. In fact, it hadn't drifted more than a mile off-shore from its original location.

That's curious, He thought.

He made a mental note to contact Lakur Industries and get all the schematics and technical information on that yacht later. It was time for his team to head home.

They received their base coordinate details from UKNI-Net. There was a secret underwater base located fifteen miles directly south of the southernmost tip of Florida. They entered the codes into the automatic piloting systems and prepared for the two-hour undersea trip.

All of the APLR's combined into one massive vessel, serpentine in shape from tip to tail, while still in the air. The leading-edge dove towards the ocean and plunged in. Down they went, down until the sun's rays no longer shook the chill from the bones. Down, down, until life had to develop another method of seeing its food and surroundings.

The serpentine vessel slid through the water barely producing a ripple. As the team drifted, their minds raced. Some even wondered what it would be like to be normal again.

Edwards, however, wondered, "Will we be normal once we wake up? Because normal is overrated."

They would deal with what life brings as it happens. That's what made them elite. Facing life and anything it threw at them without flinching from the pressure or the danger. Edwards mentally edged everyone towards sleep. Then, within seconds of confirming that everyone's vitals had reached levels ready for suspended animation, he drifted off himself.

As the island returned to its original state, the inner island extended a bridge as it opened up. Lakur and all those that had changed form walked out to greet the Dr. and the other survivors on the outer Isle.

Not long after this reunion did several stealth-sub battleships surface and send in boats to retrieve the people on the island. The human members were rounded up and moved to the submarines for debriefing. Lakur and the others were allowed to return on the Lakur yacht and were directed to an undisclosed location for confidential briefing and arrangements before they were allowed to return to their normal lives.

***

As Edwards came too, he was rather groggy. His head hurt, and his sight was blurry. Dr. Muerte was standing over him with a grim expression. He thought to himself; What's *wrong?*

Before he could voice his thoughts, Dr. Muerte answered, "We can't de-mutate you and the crew yet."

For a minute, after sitting up, Edwards simply stared blankly at Muerte. Had he been dreaming? No, he and the squad had diverted worldwide devastation. They had fought off non-Earthy beings for survival, but why weren't they back to normal???

Edwards turned toward Muerte and asked, "Why?"

Muerte pulled a remote out of his pocket. The lights went out when he hit a button, and the wall in front of where Edwards was sitting fluttered to life. It showed real-time satellite imagery of the planet Jupiter.

"What's going on Muerte? You've got some explaining to do," Edwards began with vitriol in his voice.

As Edwards was speaking, the satellite images magnified a thousand times to show an object arriving just outside of Jupiter's atmosphere. The object hovering in Jupiter's orbit; Edwards recognized as the Charcomanti spacecraft they had encountered a few days ago. While watching the video, another larger vessel of similar design emerged from the gas giants red spot. It seemed as if the two objects would collide and then the smaller one simply merged with the larger one. The object changed shape a few moments later, and the screen indicated a satellite reading depicting a tightly banded transmission of enormous power.

"What was that?" Edwards asked Muerte.

"That Commander is what our advisors consider to be a call for reinforcements." Dr. Muerte explained.

Edwards thought for a moment and then asked, "Why do you think it's a call for back up?"

Muerte looked at him and responded, "The satellites, aimed outward away from the sun on a vector from which this thing came, indicate that there is something, within two light years distance from our planet, and that distance is getting shorter, which means?"

Edwards understood and completed the statement, "Something else, is headed toward Earth!"

NOT THE END... IT'S JUST BEGINNING

About the Author

A St. Louis native, Adair grew up on the North side of St. Louis City in Missouri. An early participant of the desegregation program (a program that bussed African American students residing in the city to predominantly white populated schools in St. Louis county), he recalls spirited debates with his English teachers about the proper use of words in the dictionary.

It was that same spirit and passion that Adair started his own business as a professional photographer, later expanding his services to videography.

Adair never forgot his love of writing or his passion for words that fueled his debates as a student. Writing for years whatever the Lord inspired him to write, Mr. Rowan now writes in a myriad of genres and art forms from song and rap lyrics to spoken word and suspense or sci-fi novels. With a number of projects in the pipeline, look forward to several works from this up and coming author that include faith-based fiction, faith-based science and technology, period fiction and script writing.

Coming Soon from Adair Rowan

Project Arial, A Novel

Books by Adair Rowan

Concentric Relations – Unknown Ties

Want to know more about Adair?
Drop him a line or ask him a question on the
following social media:

Facebook: www.facebook.com/adair.rowan
Instagram: www.instagram.com/adaurophoto
Twitter: www.twipu.com/arowan89
Website: www.midwest-creations-
publishing.square.site/author-adair-rowan

Enjoyed reading Concentric Relations: Unknown
Ties?

Check out the Midwest Creations Publishing
Website for more exciting authors and books at
www.midwest-creations-publising.weebly.com or
keep reading for upcoming MWCP releases and
don't forget to sign up for the newsletter to stay
abreast of MWCP bargains, prizes, updates and
events – share this Faith-based fiction with a fun
twist with your friends and families today!

Midwest Creations Presents...

Author Chantay M. James and the Brainwaiver Universe!

What if you could have anything you desire? Is what you desire worth everything you possess – including your soul?

Waivering Minds, Book I: Brainwaiver Series

Celine:

A Licensed Clinical Social Worker in Alton, Illinois, Celine Baltimore lives a content, peaceful life. Until one of her patients reveals that her sister has become a guinea pig for behavior modification technology known as "Brainwaiver," then disappears.

Left with a child's journal that paints her once comfortable life in horror and intrigue, Celine finds herself nose deep in corporate secrets, shifty attorneys and rugged, intense men (specifically Enoch Sampson or Sam for short).

Shocked that she's named a winner in the Brainwaiver contest (a contest she'd never entered) Celine learns of more missing children in Alton and their link to the hip new software trying to take over her life; including Sam's teenaged son.

An all-around goof that can't stop tripping over her Aubusson rug (or keep said rug straight) can Celine let go of playing it safe, fight the good fight of faith and get the guy in the end?

Sam:

A widower and ex-CIA agent turned owner of a family owned construction company, Sam picked up a few skills from his former life. Some he wishes he'd never learned. Espionage and secrets had been his business.

Missions and sacrifice had become his life. Growing cold again seemed inevitable... until he met goofy (and determined) Celine Baltimore.

Could he avoid that place of unfeeling and do the unthinkable? Retrieve his son and love again? Because protecting his family was the only thing that mattered to Sam.

It was something that he would do at any cost. It was more than a goal – it was a promise. And Sampson men ALWAYS kept their promises.

Waivering Lies, Book II: Brainwaiver Series

Max:

Max Arpaio is a Freelance Information Systems Security Analyst and part time Bounty Hunter on occasion. When Max responded to Enoch Sampson's call for help to find his missing son he realized something crucial.

The top government secrets and plots he'd stumbled upon long ago are no longer a shadow on the horizon.

And Now that Denise Ferry has taken up the gauntlet to wage a silent war against Brainwaiver, Max has to make a choice: To help the woman he loves but can never have or stand aside and watch as millions are led like sheep to a slaughter. Either way, he's a dead man. It's only a question of when.

Balboa:

Denise Ferry is a Business Consultant, former FBI agent and a severe pain in Max's rear. A woman who has gone from gang member lieutenant to military strategist to agent, she could write a book on espionage and silent war strategies.

So, when Denise engaged in a search and retrieve mission that targeted children for mind control experimentation, she's in for the long haul to wage war. However, she hadn't counted on warring on two fronts: Against the advances of Brainwaiver and to win the heart of Max Arpaio.

A man of mystery with a sense of doom, Max draws Denise despite her efforts to fight the attraction. Can she help him overcome his dark past?

As a strategist she realizes she has no choice. Without him taking her back against Brainwaiver, she's already lost the war before she starts. And without him in her life she's already lost her heart.

MWCP UPCOMING RELEASES AND AUTHOR LIST:

<u>Adair Rowan</u> (Faith-based, Sci-Fi, Suspense, Science and Tech)
- **Concentric Relations: Unknown Ties** – March, 2019

Projects for **Adair**:
- **Project Ariel**

<u>Chantay M. James</u> (Faith-based Romance, Sci-Fi and Suspense)
Available to pick up your copy today:
- **Valley of Decisions** (kindle, paperback)
- **Waivering Minds, Book 1: Brainwaiver Series** (kindle, paperback)
- **Waivering Winds, Novella 1.5: Brainwaiver Series** (free for limited time!) (Mobi, PDF, EPUB)
- **Waivering Lies, Book II: Brainwaiver Series** (kindle, paperback)
- **Brainwaiver Beginnings** shorts: Wattpad (Chantay M. James)

Projects for **Chantay**:
- **Waivering Times, Novella 2.5: Brainwaiver Series** (as part of the

Anthology **WAIVERINGS** – will include novella 1.5 listed above).
- **Waivering Eyes, Book III**: Brainwaiver Series (December, 2019)
- **Gangsta Nun Series** – 2020 (spin off of Waivering Lies featuring Balboa's ex-gang gone good as activists/vigilantes)

<u>C. Marie Evans</u> (Faith-based Black Romance and Action)
New Author!!!
- **A Hater's Prayer** (June 2019)
-
- Coming Soon:
- **A Hater's Prayer 2: Annie B.'s Legacy** (May. 2020)
- **C.J. Series** – Action (2020-2022)
    o CJ Run
    o CJ Hide
    o CJ Fall
    o CJ Rise

<u>M. Renae</u> (Christian Living, Real Life)
- **Allowed 2 Cheat: A Memoir** – January, 2020

And many more authors are coming soon! Don't forget to check out the website for author swag, events and giveaways!